"James Greer is one of the nimblest and mo̶st̶
multilayered American fiction writers."

— **Dennis Cooper**, author of *Ugly Man*

"James Greer writes within the grand tradition of American
postmodern, pessimistic, philosophic geniuses. Like William Gass or
Guy Davenport, he unites sly humor, erudition, and a certain classical
cast of mind, as aware of Heraclitus as he is of Teenage Fanclub.
These stories are remarkable. They're also a total freaking blast."

— **Mathew Specktor**, author, *American Dream Machine*,
senior editor, *Los Angeles Review of Books*

"Dazzling, swirling, ridiculous and disconcerting.
James Greer doesn't follow paths, he's a thing of the air."

— **Ben Loory**, author of *Stories for Nighttime and Some for the Day*

To brand James Greer's slim new collection, *Everything Flows*,
"experimental fiction" would be to sell it painfully short.
Experimental fiction has its own rules and acceptable parameters, and
Greer, a former bassist for the band Guided by Voices, exceeds even
these over the course of these 19 urgent dispatches from the far side
of reason, where anything can occur...And yet every word matters,
even the wildest stories scarcely seeming as though they could
be otherwise. Usually this sort of free-associative reverie is called
"strange" or "playful," but Greer's lyrical erudition is both serious
work and seriously fun. Halfway between the mind of God and a
vivid dream, *Everything Flows* is proof that there remain new places to
go, both on paper and in the known universe.

— ***Publishers Weekly*** (starred review)

EVERYTHING FLOWS

Stories

By James Greer

CURBSIDE SPLENDOR PUBLISHING

This is a work of fiction. All incidents, situations, institutions, governments, and people are fictional and any similarity to characters or persons living or dead is strictly coincidental.

Published by Curbside Splendor Publishing, Inc., Chicago, Illinois in 2013.

First Edition
Copyright © 2013 by James Greer
Library of Congress Control Number: 2012951908

ISBN 978-0-9834228-8-4

Collages by Robert Pollard
www.robertpollardart.com

Designed by Shawn Stucky

Edited by Lauryn Allison Lewis

Manufactured in the United States of America.

Curbside Splendor
www.curbsidesplendor.com

"If for a particular kind of displacement of a body, as turning round an axis, the force tending to bring it back to a given position varies as the displacement, the body will execute simple harmonic vibrations about that position, the periodic time of which will be independent of their amplitude."

– James Clerk Maxwell, *Matter and Motion* (1877)

Many of these stories previously appeared, often in different form, in other publications. The author is deeply grateful to *Yeti, trnsfr, Metazen, Smokelong Quarterly, Curbside Splendor, Joyland NYC, Zaporogue, Slake Los Angeles, The Rattling Wall, On Earth As It Is, Two Letters*, Akashic Books, and *Sensitive Skin* for permission to publish those stories here.

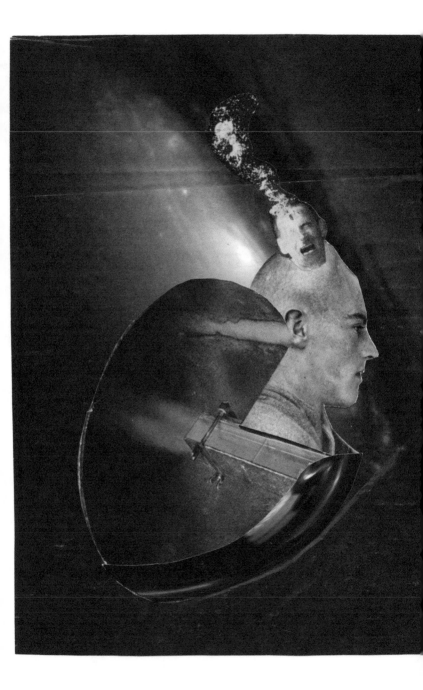

Self-Destruction, Vol. 1

I have planetary wounds. By which I mean, I move planets, and it hurts. The process of moving planets, never fun, exactly, but not without its sidereal benefits, he added, in a jocular tone to denote a joke, to subvert suspicion of pretense, because in the worst way he feared suspicion of pretense, can physically. You get bumps and bruises and mysterious cuts. These never heal.

So the question sits up like a small dog, tongue draped over teeth, whining: why do I engage in moving-planet behavior. Question mark. Answer: It is a compulsion. All right, an addiction. Never doubt your powers, is the advice I have extracted from the advisors who advise me in my business. Always doubt your powers, perhaps is a better way of putting it.

Routledge Ruut is not his real name, not even close. Anagrams are a waste of the point is. He tries and tries to see what the matter with his silly life (he knows his life is silly, so I am not "telling tales out of school"). I live in a cabin made of pine logs that does not mean it is a log cabin. The snow silts up to the windows in the wild wind: from early fall to late spring, I am unapproachable. Routledge Ruut will come to see me often in that time. He approaches by a way I have not discovered because it is profoundly uninteresting.

"Hello, Routledge Ruut," I say when he bangs on my portal. The word door is forbidden in my house. So I say portal. "What brings you to my door?" I am the only one allowed to say door, I should add.

I ask what brings Routledge Ruut only to amuse the fingers of fire that reach for the frigid air of my open portal. For no other earthly reason. Because Routledge Ruut replies the same thing every time, and wisely so, or he would not be admitted within my piney walls.

"I was in the neighborhood," he replies. I love that answer! It is the only possible answer. I throw wide the door and tug him into my cabin. One time I believe I may have flung my arms around his scarf-bedecked neck and kissed his face, repeatedly, because once you start something like kissing a man's face which is extremely cold to the point of frostbite, and your lips are warm from excellent coffee, you will have difficulty pulling away.

But that is another matter in its entirety. I am here, I have trudged — do you like the word trudge? Because I will use it a lot whether you do or not — all the way down from my cabin to this Palace Of Authority, where you do not even have decent coffee, which I find puzzling or a better word unfathomable! And the best part is I cannot help you. I am very sorry to hear that Routledge Ruut is dead. I am. Very, very sorry. There is physical pain in my ears unrelated to my planetary wounds, caused by the sound of that sentence. Also pain that has traveled to where I keep my heart — not telling you, officer!

But there is a fundamental problem with your painful sentence. Routledge Ruut is not dead. Whether you like it or not, whether it jibes with your reports and findings and autonomies and taxonomies and hysterectomies, I hate to break. To be the one to break. The thing you have cut into pieces and examined through a microcosm was not, is not, will never be Routledge Ruut.

If you bring me some real coffee I will explain or rather relate the real story. Up to you. Or you can place my cells in your cell. I really don't mind.
You choose.

That Captain is something. I believe he is a Captain, or believes himself to be a Captain, though I am unversed in the uniform insignia of the Palace Of Authority. He will not look me in the eye. I say eye because I have only one eye. Otherwise it would have been correct to say eyes. I say I have only one eye but what I mean is I only have one with me. I didn't bring the other. I travel light.

You only need one eye to move a planet. Has to be a strong eye, a good eye, but one will do. Say you're interested in placing Mars a smidge closer to the sun, because of reasons that you should and do keep private, and then what's the process? Projection, you know, planar motion, vortices, quasar pulses, etcetera. It's technical. The only hard part is when you actually arrive at the planet with the lever, which — I wish someone would explain this to me — is inevitably made from rough-hewn wood, so the splinter-effect (another technical term) plays a big role in the bumps and bruises and unhealable mysterious cuts.

You try explaining this to a Captain who won't stoop to look you in the eye. He would have to stoop, because he refuses to sit, and I am sitting. This Captain thinks I'm the one who killed Routledge Ruut. I admit I make a very good suspect in a theoretical murder. But I keep trying to tell you people, including the Captain who will not so much as look at me, Routledge Ruut is not dead. Therefore I cannot be the one who killed him. No one can be the one who killed him. Doesn't that make sense? Am I saying something, what, incoherent or non-parseable?

Thank you for the coffee. It is not much better than the last coffee but I can see you made an effort. I can taste that you made. You understand. We can go over anything you want as many times as you want. No. That I cannot do. Correction: will not do. Because my name is the only secret I have left! You know about the planetary wounds, a thing I never even showed Routledge Ruut, though I hinted at dark things. He could not have guessed I was talking about my wounds. Can you imagine? Had he been able to guess that, you'd have to call him crazy. He was a little eccentric, sure, in other words he had quirks of character, but I would not call him crazy. Crazy is a word I like to try to avoid unless you mean in a throwaway way. "That's just crazy!" No one really means that when they say that. You can talk all you want about the power of words but at the end of the day, that's just crazy.

Two days ago. To be precise, two days and one night, because he arrived at night, I mean the night before the day. Before midnight, you see what I mean? I'm not sure exactly, around 2300 hours Greenwich Mean Time. I don't know what time that is here. That's the only way I know how to tell time. I have an atomic clock I keep on the window sill next to the jar containing my other eye in a green fluorescent fluid. The atomic clock, which I made myself, is based on the half-life of American Literature. To you, to anyone without special training, the clock looks like a book. But to me it is a clock, and extremely accurate, as accurate as anything your technology can dream into action. So that was when he arrived. He left — I cannot tell you when he left. Because I left before him. I wanted to trudge through the snow and shake the branches of some pine trees. Shake the snow off the branches, I mean. The way you do, when you're young, and the snow is a kind of magic powder that grants wishes. For me, don't ask why, this still works, which is why I have to get up every morning at 1100 hours G.M.T. and go out and shake the snow off the trees and fall down laughing and covered in a shawl of snowdust. Otherwise I might lose the ability to move planets, which I wished for many years ago and received and still. So you see I'm a bit superstitious. Every morning, without fail. And when I got back to the not-log cabin, Routledge Ruut was gone.

Not long gone, no. The fire had been recently stoked. He had not made coffee because he wouldn't dare. He knew better than to touch the coffee machine I designed myself from the spare parts of — let's just say of other things. I am the only one who knows how to operate the coffee machine, and I am the only one, consequently, who is allowed to operate the coffee machine. As a general rule. I believe that general rules, if adopted broadly across the planets, would make things run more smoothly and the product of the worker's labor would be higher quality. Maybe the highest, though how can you measure something like highest quality. Highest compared to what?

I'm sorry, I know, off topic. I tend to do that. Alone most of the time you see. Not much used to company. So, okay, he must have left sometime after 1100 hours G.M.T. but before 1145 hours G.M.T., at almost exactly which time I returned to the cabin and brushed as well as I could all the particles of snow still clinging to my wool jacket and gloves and knitted ski cap, sea-green, and my blue jeans and rugged, well-worn work boots. I performed these brushings on the porch, of course, and removed my work boots and pushed open the portal and stepped into the cabin in my thick plaid socks of which I keep exactly three pair. I don't see why that's any of your business.

Think about what you're asking. Moving on from the socks business. How could I be expected know where or in what direction Routledge Ruut trudged away from my cabin of not-logs? I am not a tracker. I can't tell an Arctic silver fox from a winter hare. Are those animals? Actual animals or invented by automobile companies? You can't ever tell, in my opinion.

His footsteps, my footsteps. I'm sure you have sensitive infra-spectrum machines that can determine minute differences in body weight, distribution, height, hair color, number of tooth extractions, simply from the tread of a well-worn work boot. So you already know more than I know in this regard. Incidentally, interesting story, my father, who had not been to the dentist in forty years, recently had five tooth extractions in a single sitting. Could I have another pour of this mediocre coffee? Could I trouble you? Be careful what you agree. Be. That's all I'm. Thank you.

Instead of listening to my story I think we could be more productive here if you were to tell me yours. So I know what I'm up against. Do I have that right, or did I waive when. Okay, perhaps as a courtesy? Otherwise we will be here all day dealing with irrelevant details. That's my job, or a part of my job. And I'm good at my job. Help me to help me.

Let's start with where, the place, you say you found Routledge Ruut, lying face down in a bloody puddle. The middle of your Main Street. Opposite the Post Office, from which "reliable witnesses" spotted him exiting. Here's an observation, I don't know whether it's germane: "witness" and "witless" are only one letter apart. Again, my job. All right. So then a man of roughly my build wearing roughly my clothes, except without well-worn work boots on his feet but standing — and this was such a curious detail several people noticed — in his socks, shoeless, and his socks were thick plaid socks of the type I have previously described as belonging to me, produced a shotgun and cut down Routledge Ruut with three precisely-aimed blasts, in the back. An ugly incident, no doubt. A deeply-scarring incident for those unfortunate witnesses.

From there the story gets more and less straightforward. I was approached by a member of the Palace Of Authority. I admit that I was standing shoeless in the middle of your Main Street holding a recently-fired shotgun in my left hand. No, you're right, that doesn't look good, but as I'm sure your wife would remind you, looks aren't everything. That's her in the picture on your desk, right? Lovely woman. Does she understand that the only reason you cheat on her with the barmaid at Central Tavern three times a month is because you secretly believe she finds you repulsive? That was just a guess. I don't even know if there's a place called Central Tavern. I almost never come to town.

Fine. I'll just sit here, then.

Captain, my Captain. Sorry. I'll try to be serious. It's hard to be serious in an unserious world, don't you agree, Captain. That's why I spend so much time on other worlds. Jupiter, for example, very serious place. No room for error. I think the sheer mass has something to do with that. Jupiter just has so much gravity.

There I go again. Thanks for agreeing to. It was entertaining talking to some of your officers but we both know there wasn't much chance of getting anywhere useful. Not with them. Little reflections of a big idea.

My first question, before you start in: why am I here? No, no don't answer, I'm sorry. Never question authority. You're unhappy with me. I don't blame you. I should have made the coffee before I went out to shake the trees, but I forgot. One time, I forgot. I should think my credit, my good will account, was enough to offset any offense occasioned by my neglect in this matter. Clearly not. Okay, yes, I said clearly not. You don't have to repeat everything I say, though you can if you want, you are after all the Captain, and I am your prisoner. In French I believe that's prisonnier. Probably not, huh? [NB: prisonnier is correct, although captive could be used, but would be rather less common]

Your move, Cap. I'm quite sure you haven't gone to all this trouble on my account, so I'm wondering towards what end. Surely not force me to give up secrets to your flunkies. And since there's really only one secret, surely you don't think. Because you, of all people on all worlds, and I use the term people loosely, and I grip the term worlds tightly, know that I will never vouchsafe or divulge. Because that was the deal I made, the promise kept. And you know that: because the deal I made, the promise kept, was with you, dear Captain.

Do you want to see the wounds? I can't think of any other reason, though I know reason isn't big on your list of priorities, not that you have an actual list. You can move planets as easily as I can. Easier, actually, having created them. You can do anything, as I understand it. You invented anything. You invented not only the possible but the impossible, and decided which was which, and decided who would be allowed to operate outside the lines of your coloring book.

I will show you the wounds, then. Here, on my hands. No, the palms. You have to look closely. If you press on the scar blood sort of oozes from the edges. That's what I mean they never heal. Hold on, I'll pull up my pant leg. See that? That's from the moon. Dark side. Nasty place if you don't watch out. I had both eyes in and still: Mare Tranquilis my ass.

This can't be all. I told your people nothing, nothing. I did not tell them your real name, even. You said always use the pseudonym, and once again I have kept my promise. So here I sit, accused of killing your pseudonym. Is that a crime? Murder of a name? Really? Honestly?
I didn't know. Yes, ignorance of the law is no.

I'm stunned, a bit. I admit I did not think this was real. I didn't take it seriously. I didn't understand the magnitude of. I suppose I should make a full confession. I am guilty. I am guilty. I am guilty. What is it they say in the Catholic Church? Mea maxima culpa.

Why are you crying? No one knows that you are Routledge Ruut. Or used to be, before I killed him. Your secret is safe.

Oh. I hadn't thought of punishment. Is that really necessary? Stupid question. Crime and punishment. Coincidentally, the name of my atomic clock.

What do you mean why did I do it? You told me. You instructed — you *commanded* me to do it. So who's being punished here? Or rather, who ought to be punished? Mover of worlds or creator of mover of worlds. Stop crying, it's attracting attention. Of course I love you. Of course I would die for you. These are silly. It's not worth getting worked up.

No. I'm not going to run. First of all run where? Venus? Have you been to Venus recently? Unpleasant's putting it mildly. Plus it's just too hot, you can't get anything done, it's torpid. Like Miami in summer times a hundred. And don't say Uranus, that's beneath you.

I will stay. I will accept my punishment. Anything else would be unjust. You know it, I know it, that guy over there stroking his beard and watching us with his one good eye — he especially knows. Do not tempt me, Captain. I have turned down better offers than yours.

Yes, he explained my rights. He explained everything. I am satisfied that due process has been followed in every respect of my case. As it turns out, the Captain is a very open and courteous fellow, once you get to know him. Very up front. Answered a lot of my. So the sooner, I think, we get on with the procedure the better. Good.

Guilty.

Do I have a choice as to method?

I choose the third thing he said. Do I have a choice as to time?

Can you please translate that into G.M.T.? Thank you. I choose what you would call dawn, then. How long does that give me to prepare? Fine. I will take it now. Give me a glass of water.

No, I don't want a priest. You would not call a butcher to perform heart surgery. Sorry. I don't mean to be rude. You've all been very professional, to say the least. Please leave me now.

Captain, I know you're listening. I can't see you but I know you can see me. I'm very sad, Captain. I did not expect this sadness. Nor this fear. Swinging from Saturn's rings was never so scary as the prospect of annihilation, and I could not tell you why. I will miss Saturn's rings, by the way. They are beautiful. Good job there. I'll miss your visits to my cabin, made of pine logs but not a log cabin, because the logs were chopped and planed and sawed by your hand, using hand as a metaphor I suppose. Won't you miss my coffee? My kisses? The conversation about stars and planets and galaxies, some that you had seen or made that I would never see, or at least now will never see. Why do you make the end so difficult, Captain? Is that on purpose? To test our faith? Oh, and who will move the planets now that I am gone?

Life a leaf. Falls like the long snow of winter's end. I see, said the blind man, as he picked up his hammer and saw.

Cellini's Salt-Cellar

The Sea is represented by a figure of Man, the Earth by a figure
of Woman. The legs of the two figures are intertwined, the way
the artist imagined the limbs of land and sea are conjoined. Ten
thousand gold crowns were melted to supply the metal from which
these two figures are cast, or rather molded free-hand from rolled
gold. The gold has been covered in enamel in some parts, and
there is a base, too, carved from ebony and adorned with more
figures, meant to represent the four winds, the times of day, and
emblems of human activity. To the Sea's right is a golden ship,
intended to hold salt. To the Earth's right is a golden temple,
intended to hold pepper. The finished item, which took four
years and the labor of many workshop assistants to complete, was
commissioned by the King of France, Francis I, in 1540. From his
possession the salt-cellar passed to King Charles IX and then to
Archduke Ferdinand, an Austrian, which is how in due course the
piece ended up at the Kunsthistorisches Museum in Vienna, KK
Inv. No. 881.

An old man writes the story of his life into a book. In the
story he presents himself as hero, the fulcrum of the world, fording
a torrent of troubles, and receiving for his pains the envy of his
peers and a comforting foretaste of immortality. He tells the
world he's the greatest goldsmith in history, and so he becomes
the greatest goldsmith in history. He tells the world that his art
has raised him to the level of divine Michelangelo, and the world
places his name alongside Michelangelo, and Da Vinci, and
anyone else he cares to suggest. He has outsmarted Popes, and
out-dueled princes, and reaped from the courts of kings his just
reward in riches and praise. An extraordinary character, his story
encompasses the spirit of an age: its devotion to transcendence
in all things, especially beauty, and more especially in aesthetic
accomplishment.

Over time, the examples the old man provides or references
in the book of his work -- his enduring, fame-bestowing,
unparalleled artistry -- disappear one by one. Some are melted
down for use as coinage in currency-starved principalities, some
are destroyed accidentally, some on purpose, some succumb to
age or weather, some simply fall out of fashion and are moved

from backroom to backroom, acquiring a lacquer of grime their maker never foresaw. The sculpture, or plate, or fountain, or bust, is forgotten, is lost, has unmade itself through some unknown agency of fate.

So that at present, and for a very long time now indeed, the only evidence of our artist's prowess is this salt-cellar. And this book -- yes, the book, because unlike the goldsmith's artifacts he trumpets with immodest vigor, the book survives. More than survives: the book remains one of the most popular literary works from the period we still call the Renaissance. Popular, perhaps, for a reason that its author had not intended: for its catholic view of the social lives of those we would otherwise little know. The author does not stoop to ignore the least significant detail of his life, out of faith that future generations will be instructed or entertained by his example. We have feuds with innkeepers and insults traded with mountebanks and a parade of whores and grubby business dealings with the disreputable commercial classes who would eventually inherit the earth. We have, in short, a vivid, panoramic account of a time and a place inaccessible to us, which teaches that even the great and lordly artists of the Renaissance had lives not dissimilar to our own. And if that is true, then all things are possible. In the end, therefore, the author's greatest extant achievement -- the one, at least, responsible for whatever measure of immortality he will retain in the memory of humankind -- is the one over which he took least pains.

We invite you now to look at the salt-cellar, sole remaining example of the goldsmithing genius of Benvenuto Cellini. It is remarkable. Remarkable. A true work of art.

Everything Flows

Alphonse Samson stood before the mirror in his bathroom for
a long time before deciding to. The mirror had no frame but its
edges were beveled and the soft light from the neighbor's bright
room shining through a small square heavy-glass window above
his head on the right wall produced a doubling of. The scissors, he
concluded after staring at them longer than was necessary to arrive
at such a conclusion, were too small. He would need. He put the
scissors on the back left edge of the ceramic sink and opened the
medicine cabinet by pulling on the right edge of the mirror, which
was hinged. Inside were four bottles of prescription drugs, all of
which remained sealed. To deal with the problem later. To ignore,
as long as possible, the ill effects.

There were three outcomes, and none of them. Anything
else was a reflection only, the shadow of action. According to his
disintegrating paperback of *At-Swim-Two-Birds,* [TK quote at
very end of book which you stole and re-purposed for the end
of *Artificial Light*]. Or to put it differently, as TK had done in
TK *Voyages en Afrique,* and obviously Roussell's [sp?] *Voyages en
Afrique* [check both these references, obviously the books weren't
called the same thing or even either of those things, but there was
"Afrique" in the title of both, or at least in my memory there was,
which is the point], the which both of which to say precisely the
same thing but in different ways and. In the pile of books on his
office desk. The photo of James Joyce walking along the strand
in Dublin he had framed and propped on the desk against the
yellowing wall. The photo of Nabokov reading by lamplight which
he had framed and propped against the pale green wall next to
the photo of Joyce. Most people assumed these were relatives. Is
that your grandfather. Yes I said yes it is. [May have used this joke
more than one too many times.]

In France they call scotch tape le scotch. For a long time
Alphonse used to go to bed early, but then he finished the final
volume of *In Search of Lost Time* and there seemed no point. He
started going to bed a little later, maybe ten o'clock instead of
eight-thirty or nine, but he still woke up without fail at five in the
morning. This was the best time of day for getting things done.
The most productive. This was the most productive part of the day.

For Alphonse, the early morning hours were. There was a wasp buzzing a wasp buzzed outside of his office window buzzed a wasp or possibly a bee [can one tell by timbre of buzz? check] whose low hum sounded like an old man talking on the phone, or to himself, about something private. As if there were words just under the threshold. A kind of meaning. Like the amnion of unbirthed sun the pregnant dark from which the filigree of colors from which soon would burst the slow heat from it would soon be dawn. The desk lamp produced a semi-circle a circle a half circle a crescent of silvery light shone silvery light on silvered light on the small stack of books and the worn wood of his desk. There was also a paperweight a round paperweight with a bird a black bird looking at red at red holly berries on a branch against a yellow background and a silver heart-shaped box containing in which could be found a pewter heart-shaped container an ornate, beaded box in the shape of a heart with a heart embossed on its lid which when opened contained revealed a polished pink quartz heart in a blue velvet lining lined with blue velvet the box was lined with blue velvet and contained a smoothly polished pink rose pink quartz heart. Index cards and sticky notes and nearly twenty pens of various kinds and multi-colored pens of various types: ball point and felt-tipped and. A pencil-sharpener, electric, and a three hole punch, manual. The pewter box containing the rose pink stone heart was a gift from Caeli Fax from whom Alphonse had received many gifts and.

The walls of the office were lined with books arranged haphazardly arranged in no particular order disorder desultory disarray that followed a system only he could understand because he had invented the system of his own design which he had himself invented in fact was a system there was in fact a system behind the disorder a method. [Not a method.] C. M. Bowra's book on Heroic Poetry was next to nestled against Richardson's Clarissa which itself in order you could find C. M. Bowra's volume on Heroic Poetry, Richardson's Clarissa, Burton's *Anatomy of Melancholy* [not that again you are always using it or misusing it in fact] *The Poetical Works of Shelley, Stephen Hero* by James Joyce [no you have a picture of him on the desk that would be too obvious something better like *The Journal of Albion Moonlight*], Mao's Little Red Book, and Newton's *The Principia* [doesn't that have a longer title in other words didn't he write more than one Principia but on different subjects for Christ's sake you have a Ph.D. in physics you ought to know these things this is one of the worst aspects of aging is when your memory goes. I used to be able to picture everything as in a photograph, I used to refer to my memory as eidetic "but only when I drink" hilarious you stupid fuck now it would be better described as idiotic… eidetic, idiotic. Not the worst *jeu de mots*. Why does Barth always use such bad French in his books? He uses a lot of French, too, in every book there's some little snippet of French either appropriated or appropriate to the scene. *The Sot-Weed Factor* that chapter where they go confront the Jesuit or the secret Jesuit and Burlingame in disguise speaks to him in French to prove his bona fides but the French is completely wrong. Almost Google Translate level wrong. As if he didn't care. Or didn't know any better. At least he didn't have the excuse of relying on Google Translate as it didn't exist back then but whatever high school or college (should these be capitalized?) level courses he may have taken did not stick. UNLESS the awkward or just incorrect French is deliberate, in which case it is always deliberate, down to his last book latest most recent book novel *Every Third Thought* where he makes elemental masculin-feminin errors. That would be a device were it the case, but even as device towards what end?]

Godard's Histoire(s) *du Cinéma* apparently has been or is going to be released on Region One DVD this year. Finally. The Artificial Eye UK version is very good of course but you can't turn off the English subtitles which is frustrating. The greatest achievement [maybe] in film ever and you can't watch it the way it was intended and the subtitles don't add anything on top of which they're distracting. Also it plays in the wrong aspect ratio on every all-region player I own. Presumably a Region One version would play in the correct aspect ratio. And the transfer could use some work, too, though having been produced for television I doubt the image quality can be improved drastically. The constant bombardment [word choice] of image and text and sound, the layering, the incredible montages, these. What the fuck is Kombucha anyway? What exactly is it supposed to do for you? *Bacillus coagulans* GBI-30 6086: 1 billion. S. Boulardi: 1 billion. 1 billion what? Units? Strands? Molecules? Bacteria? And why would

I want to put 2 billion anythings into my gut and since I have apparently done just that what is going to happen to me? Will I get any of my memory back? Will it rewrap the frayed synapses in my gray matter? It will not no it won't it will at best one can expect it will produce noisy eructations. The which I may well have produced independent of the 2 billion somethings or other that I recently introduced to my body.

And a stapler, also manual. The stapler was Alphonse's most prized possession partly mostly due to its longevity: he had stolen it from an office where he had worked as a clerk when he was sixteen and the staples as well which he still had, in boxes, in the bottom drawer of a credenza from probably Ikea [try to stay away from brand names, in twenty years Ikea is not going to mean anything, it's like saying "Xxxxxxxx Xxxxxxxx" already nobody remembers that band, and rightly so, awful band, if only that he had hired a singer instead of trying to sing himself. No one else in the band could play except the drummer, so why not be satisfied with over-dubbing forty-thousand guitar parts and writing simplistic not-great melodies to go with your reductive me versus the world lyrics and have someone who can sing do the singing?]. The staples were in their original boxes of blue-and-white cardboard, 5000 staples each in long rows stacks of rows of 500 each and had not rusted or lost their appeal over years [see that? it's your nose. And this is sitting on top of it] nor had the stapler ever required maintenance. Alphonse would not argue with anyone who said that things in general used to be better made constructed more sturdily built to last because in his experience or at least in his experience as regards as concerns regarding the stapler that was true the case more often than not. He was in the habit of drawing general conclusions from specific knowledge which is why the world has become is becoming will become a dark and savage place.

He squinted at his reflection in the mirror. All things in this best of all possible. In his left hand a weight, a thing with weight, an object that weighed. His fingers curled around the. People say now or never but that's not. Never is an awfully long time. From the monochrome streetlights of Alphaville to the tangerine night sky in Alphabet City to the dusty unripe brown pear lid over Los Angeles and back and forth we go up. We go down. To be or not to be is false equivalence. Not every answer is binary. Between being and nothingness stretches a fantail of options, each with the same consequence with a different consequence the same completely different similar result and the end is the end after all is never the end. A golden spiral trapped in a glass paperweight with a black bird looking at red berries against a yellow background and you bring the object to your throat and squeeze but suppose but I suppose thought Alphonse that having made it this far there are as many compelling arguments pro as contra, in the absence of absolutes which we may take as granted or at least for purposes of argument granted by deficit by the God.

To be able, for all and ever, to stop explaining oneself. To stop justifying, excusing, apologizing, lying above all lying. To stop. To stop talking. There is in every human heart an impulse towards irony that is both the making and unmaking of us. No other animal can act irrationally on purpose. Can self-harm knowing the damage that will be done. Can drive at high-speed into the ass-end of an alley full-stopped by a brick wall, on a motorcycle, without a helmet, in Paris, because just because.

Alphonse Sampson cut his jugular with a razor three times and scrawled with a dying hand on the mirror good-bye, good-bye, good-bye.

The Decision Tree

Prologue

Low light slants through a bower of maple branches onto the roof and dirt-spattered windshield of a car parked on the red clay driveway. No wind stirs, and the mosaic of shadow slides by imperceptible degrees from the blue roof of the parked car to the tawny drive, crawling from there to the tips of the trees. Cinders of sunset spark on the windshield between buttons of grime. On the porch of the adjacent house, a large dog sleeps restlessly, its black ears twitching in the evening heat, next to a swing hung between white wooden columns. Through the grid of windows facing the porch, a woman stirring sauce in the kitchen presents an occasional profile, hair pulled back neatly and rubber-banded, brow flexed in thought. She stops stirring and lifts the spoon to her lips, one hand cupped beneath, bending her neck forward slightly to greet the upwards curve of the spoon-bearing hand.

My cigarette smoke rising from an empty chair on the porch mirrors the steam from the sauce, twining in the window, which reflects not only the warm light from the kitchen but the sun's quiet death. The first few fireflies test their turn signals, harbingers of impending night. One buzzes too close to the sleeping dog, inducing a drastic shift in the stubborn flow of time and place: the dog yawns, and suddenly I'm in a dark room in a cold city with a streetlight blaring in my eyes. Impermanence, I have a feeling, is a self-inflicted wound.

1. Absence

It's cold in here. The window is loose in its frame and rattles with every gust of wind. I can feel the wind through my sweater, slowly unraveling like the frayed edges of my personality, falling apart now that I'm alone, now that no one else is around to give me substance and meaning. Outside the glare of another's perception, I'm afraid I have no real being. I'm an accretion of foreign fluid— the sweat and saliva I've sucked out of you and everyone else. That equals me. That's my sum.

Without you I have no memory, and without memory people are little better than husks. I can no longer draw your face in my mind: I remember only plangent recombinations of light and shade, half-shimmers of reflected recollection, spangles of recognition—as if you were mirrored in a poorly lit store window, at an oblique angle, on one of my memory's byways or side streets. I'm starting to forget what everything looks like. My room is inhabited by phantoms of objects I'm sure I long ago lost, and the shapes of the few things that do remain seem to shift from moment to moment. I'm constantly bumping into my table and spilling books onto the floor, books I didn't even know I had and certainly have never read, nor will.

Hunger and thirst are feminine. *Ho fame, ho sete.* Do you hunger and thirst after righteousness, or do you, as I do, simply hunger and thirst, in the most obvious and humiliating ways? A penny shines on my dresser, reflecting the tangerine streetlight outside the window. I want that coin's brightness, its permanence, its lack of permanence. Everything.

Time's been severed at the root, lopped, trimmed and sent spinning from space by a single brutal blow. Poor gap-toothed infinite, our silly sun, useless armies of stars in her fingerless hands. Garlands and garlands of two-lipped truths dangle from her neck. Who collects the residue of passion?

2. Presence

Liquid syllables spill down the phone lines, like wet diamonds, like a wild boar in a shadow forest. Message from a seasick heart. The sun in my blood goes supernova and gutters out. The moon, I'm beginning to think, has designs on me. The moon has a motive. I've felt the lunar tug before, but never so strong, never so pure. Every atom in me vibrates with its light, and I lie unmoving, pinned to the bed, barely blinking. A jacaranda tree outside my window, spindly with age, bends in the moonlit wind, directing my eyes, my hands, my heart towards the image inhabiting the center of my mind.

I know what the moon wants. I know and resist with an automatic strength. I know because I can see her: sometimes she lies breathing quietly in the next room, her long and lovely fingers clutching the edges of a borrowed blanket. I envy that blanket's easy embrace, and resent the rasp of sheets against my flushed skin. Lead-limbed on my glimmering bed, I smoke a stale cigarette, exhaling with effort, and imagine the shadows falling across her face. Shadow fingers, shadow lips, shadow kisses. I'm no stranger to the rapture of attraction, but this is different. This is a matter of tides, of gravity. Of ineluctable force.

What is love? Movement of the soul towards its essential nature. All words become one word. When you say the word your life begins. If. L'if. Life. In the strange geometry of ardor, words are never proof enough.

Epilogue

Today and tomorrow, no more. Whatever pain you have caused in the past: redacted. Nothing ensues, transpires: happens. Sadness: no more. In the sky, drifting ashes mix with snow and become snow, and fall, in wet flakes, on the international date line. Let's get out of the house. Let's open the high oak doors and walk outside, breathing new air. The ice ages but we do not: no more. A blue jay carries an almond in its beak, hopping along the crooked fence. The warped and rotting boards of the fence bear the weight of the bird, and the falling snow, without complaint.

The Light That Draws The Flower

1. p. 34 Naturalism

The light that draws the flower makes a gift of the present. The river stretches drowsy limbs across gray hills, tinged with pink light from dropping sun. Anna walks through a narrow field bordered on all sides by sycamore, oak, maple, honey locust, birch, walnut, white pine, catalpa, tulip poplar, beech, linden. The tops of trees flecked with pale yellow light, but the meadow darkens quickly. Her way is plotted by fireflies, in phosphorescent bunches, dipping below the tall grass, pausing on the stalks, circling, semaphoring secrets. Lampyridae: *The firefly light is called a "cold light" because it produces almost no heat. It is produced when oxygen, breathed in through the abdominal trachea, combines with a substance called luciferin in the presence of the enzyme luciferase, in special cells called photocytes.* The tall grass parts as she walks, neck bent slightly out of sadness, out of being tired from walking for hours. Heat of day disperses in the grass, in the wildflowers growing in clumps. On the edge of the meadow, where the trees begin, mist pools in the undergrowth. Anna reaches the pooling mist and wades through, unhesitant.

Until I don't know where I am.

Anna threads through the undergrowth: ferns, dead tree parts, bluebells, decaying leaves, jack-in-the-pulpit, mossy stumps, dark stones. A cabbage butterfly arcs across her path, disappears. Fireflies are fewer, less frantic. Through the mist you can see their tiny lanterns bobbing on invisible silk threads.

Step on a twig or stick or dead root: cracks. Cold air swarms behind the mist: with sun gone, temperature cellars. After the fireflies fade Anna stops walking, gathers by feel enough wood for a fire. Clears a circle in the dirt with her feet, lays stones along the edge, piles the wood in the center. Leaves and dry bark for kindling. Produces from a mesh compartment in her backpack a box of wooden matches. The light from a struck match burns blue, then yellow orange, then blue again when applied to the leaves. Bright spurt and a sharp pop as air pockets snap to greet eager flame. She hunches near, tending with a stripped branch. Throws the branch aside, pulls backpack open. Unzips and sorts through contents, pulling out toiletries kit; sifts through kit for compact mirror. Moves strands of hair from face with aid of mirror, reflections of firelight on forehead reflected in mirror.

My face is smudged. I have some tissues, and a thing of water.

Puts away mirror and roots through backpack.

The light from the sun is different from firelight, and yet both are forms of light, and forms of heat. I draw both from both. Fiery sparks leap from the center of the turning world. Some catch on breezes or drafts of heated air and float, dangle, dip, soar, plummet.

"Hello, Anna." These are words addressed to me. Anna. O Hell. Semi-palindromic is not a thing? Is a thing?

Turns towards the voice. "I'm not alone."

"Don't count on that, Anna. Why are you here? Why run?"

"Not running."

Past the shapes of positive space grading into negative space. Can't see a bloodless thing. "Who are you? What do you want?"

"I want to help. If you'll let me."

"Who's me?"

Leaves wrestle in the dark, a twig's thin limb snaps. Long pause of just the fire noising the night.

"I'm afraid." Say a thing, it's no longer true.

"Yes. We're both afraid, Anna. What draws me here is fear. Mine and yours."

"Will you come where I can see you?"

"I could, but I think I won't."

"If I guess your name will you come near?"

"You can't. Even if you guessed right, I'd change my name before you could say out loud."

Anna pushes her backpack into position as a pillow, stretches her legs near the fire.

"Go to sleep, Anna. I won't hurt you. I won't even touch you."

"Not sleeping. Just stretching out."

"Aren't you tired?"

"Yes. But I have trouble sleeping even at home in bed. Never mind in the forest with an invisible possibly malevolent lurker chatting away."

"Something's bothering you."

"You're bothering me. I came here to not talk. And now I'm talking." Could be a wood sprite or grendel or anything, or nothing.

"Anyway I'm not invisible. I'm hiding. Like you."

"Why do you say hiding."

"No one comes to the forest for any other reason."

She closes her eyes and watches flickers of fire on the inside of vibrating eyelids. Mob of crickets mouthing off in the brush. Owl hoots over the insect din, bass clarinet riding above string section.

Minutes pass in this way.

Boys want to possess. Works out because girls want to be possessed. World goes on, possessed and abandoned and chased and possessed.

"I think that's oversimplifying."

"How oversimplifying."

"The part about the difference between boys and girls. In matters of love, right? I don't think you can generalize like that."

"How are you able to know thoughts I haven't spoken."

"You're translucent in that light, Anna. Anyone can see inside your pretty head."

Fire wants poking.

"Anyone."

Fire wants poking. Anna grabs branch, leans towards logs, turns one over so its glowering face shows.

She retracts the branch, its tip charred from flame, sets it next to her. Draws knees up to chin.

"Don't you think you're awfully precocious for a girl your age?"

"I've always been precocious."

"Always? What do you mean? A person can't always be precocious, unless he's born talking, which has never happened, and therefore can't happen, because it's unrealistic, and animals of the fortress are arriving to devour the mechanical marvels! Lo, the fendes say so! A holly jolly folly molly trolley collie.

Marvelous thing, falling asleep. Surrender to an army of nothing.

2. p. 36 Symbolic Island

Prologue: Bloating through the floodstream. Common Snowberry, Velvetleaf, Yellow Rattlebox, Bush Pea, Oconee Bells, Milkwort, Alumroot, Wood Sorrel. Frostweed, Toadshade,

Figwort, Purple Trillium, Rosy Twisted-Stalk, Teasel, Speedwell, Hyacinth, Pickerelweed, Gentian, Foam Flower, Common Moonseed, False Solomon's Seal.

Act I: In back of the deserted manse there grew a tangle of untamed shrubbery (wisteria, lilac, azalea), weeds, wildflowers (snapdragon, tickseed, beebalm, aster, hollyhock, heliotrope, cornflower), and, unexpectedly, roses, among which, according to season, bloomed a Black Jade miniature rose and several rogue Hybrid Teas (Crimson Glory, Double Delight, Fragrant Cloud, Mr. Lincoln) and a cream-white single bloom Sombreauil Tea. The Rose Garden at City Center's Botanical Complex was a desert of thorns next to our backyard's accidental rosaceae.

The property was now held in trust for an absentee owner who was in no apparent hurry to sell. Its last resident -- Oscar Siebenthaler, an old-growth German immigrant -- had been an amateur horticulturist, which explained the proliferation of flora, but in the ten years since his occupation (ended, as with many things, by death) his carefully organized garden had exploded, migrating willy-nilly over the two acres of partially wooded property. In areas thickly shaded by trees, flowers that flourished in shade grew. In sunny spots grew heliophilic things. Where conditions were right (neither too much nor too little sun, for instance up near the house itself) a scumble of colors occurred in Spring, attracting swarms of bees and butterflies -- among these: Silver-spotted Skippers (*Epargyreus clarus clarus*) and American Coppers (*Lycaena phlaes americana*) -- in abundance.

No one had an interest in clearing away the dead brush from the back yard or mowing the front or back -- as a result wild grasses flourished, which proved a boon to insects and to the birds who fed on them (Acadian Flycatcher, Barn Swallow, Horned Lark, Red-Eyed Vireo, Cedar Waxwing, as well as the usual sparrow, house wren and starling crowd). The unkempt grounds and the general disrepair of the building's facade (paint cracked and flaking, gutters askew, unhinged shingles, broken flagstones on the path leading up to the front porch, which featured a porch swing as rotted and tenuous as the gazebo across from the Belle) kept neighbors tut-tutting and most strangers at bay.

Act II: Glossy grey leaves trilling in stiff pre-thunderstorm gusts. Each tree a book read by a giant, wildly turning pages. The trunk of that old oak supports a fat bestseller. Quercus: A Romance. Anna withdrew from the warehouse of unused memories an image of her mother in a light blue print dress patterned with white-and-yellow daisies, hanging pale green sheets on a clothesline in the morning sun. The scattered flapping sound then was the same feeling as the tendrils of many trees whipped by the wind, now. She walked with hands jammed into the pockets of her jeans, slowly. Open-mouthed street has terrible teeth, crooked, uneven, discolored. Should see a dentist. How administer anesthetic? Road drools.

Act III: In every pair one is one and the other the other. One longs to fly high and the other to plug away, inventing complexities. See those complexities as necessary for sustaining and bearing life. Price for flight always clipped wings, everyone knows this but can't help *demandait des ailes*. Icarus, the one with the syncopated life.

Act IV: We still say descent of night or nightfall. Thus in Homer: "Bright light of sun sank into the ocean, dragging down dark night." Thus in Cato: "Se nox praecipitat." In the *Book Of the Dead* the red of sunset is the blood of Ra as he hastens to his suicide. To the poetic vision of early seers the crimson west seemed ensanguined by some great massacre that had been perpetrated there. Hommel & Hilprecht (Die Insel der Seligen) have identified the gateway through which Gilgamesh (the bright Day-God) had to make his way to the West: "the Twin Peaks" of Central Arabia, the mountain of Sunset, now called Jebel Shammar. Two peaks, Aga and Salama, stand apart confronting each other, and form a sort of natural portal. Egyptian representation of the sky as a great dome resting on two pillars, Shu & Tefnut. Tum-Ra, the evening sun, sets in darkness; he seizes these pillars and overthrows the sky. Aborigines of Australia believe the sky to be supported on props which keep it from falling. (This is an almost perfectly universal idea.) "It is these pillars the blinded giant (the dim-grown sun of evening) withdraws when he brings night down upon the world in the final catastrophe which involves his own death." Smythe-Palmer. Samson, bound between the twin pillars of the temple at Gaza -- enraged, blinded (in actual fact blind only in one eye, although this is not recorded in the Bible but can be demonstrated through myth-redaction -- the sun one eye, the moon in the other) -- shakes the pillars until the roof collapses, killing himself and far more Philistines, in death, than he had ever killed in life. Likewise the Sun God, (Shamesh, Shu, Gilgamesh, etc.), blinded and enfeebled by the encroaching dusk, pulls down the twin towers of the firmament at day's end, and sky collapses into night. The sun sets in the West. Rises in the East.

3. p. 236/7 Apathy in the ranks.

See: condescension, arrogance, life on the mountaintop, airless, sterile, and lonely. See further: snowfall, a small cabin with fireplace, burning, the curl of smoke pearl-gray against the whiter sky, a history book, the end of time.

    I agree.
    Now you're agreeing for its own sake. You're trying to pacify me.
    I agree.
    You're not even listening.
    I agree.

Hate disease of intuition. Resolution No. 6: *If happiness is the goal of living, then we are doomed, because we are not selfish enough by nature.*

4. p. 251 Defiance

    Matador manhandles minotaur. By the window -- sycamore, sycamore, rock. Praise be to God for addled things, for piebald sodden brains dappled with alcoholic insight. Oh, and the smooth circuitous way she lies. Incunabula of moot resistance. You cant untangle threads of mein herr, nor plum the death of sea's own sad light.
    Broken day, sepia-tint. Last falling down myth: sacrament of marriage. Linnaeus caroling through Lapland -- reindeers' balls, hags' pudenda. Sun sags to bed, world-weary, unfortunate. Moves on the face of the waters. Paraclete.
    Make lines of light where no face has ever peered, seen, sunk, drooled, wept, wiping tears with hand maid of light, lettered in

green ink, shining, like raggened blankets of green rushes, burny, reflex in scratch of optics of glasses.

Twig on this, fragment. You shard of sense. You, shorn pal. Open the dregs to the uni-drunk tri-corn. "I'll have you know. I will." René Dubois (Jules), bacteriologist. His last girlfriend, in the meaning you mean in the meaning: even, morn, day flouring, on her face and over the dour, everywhour. Travel swell.

O shore.

O lift us all, hymn.

Philomel. Singer in the eye. Ten vocabularies scumbled inner hello, stippled wit black inc. Octagonal runs to seed or runny plum. Inappropriate name, muser. Inaccurately dressed. Missed her. Moralist anger, more and less, strung along the hinge of reason, blossoms bright in rage. Time sit. Truth ache. Come put her, thousand calculations, thousand ships, face launched, rite in the center.

High and holy hill. On it grows the guts and morning glory.

King Ibn, thin. Littoral translation.

Winter harrows the land, harrowing winds dump hurricane sugar on highlands like croppings of snow. O deer, the beauty and the bees. Notting hear.

Again, aging. Trump.

Ace.

Aces.

Access.

Ate.

In the Latin, lads, its ove for egg, in Eytie dove for where, in Angleterre Dover for endall beall. Lovers leap. Lovers leap, lads, and you shall leap.

You shall leap.

5. p. 368 Animal/Man

Ridiculous theories about dancing bees and color vision. Might hoodwink the academy and the Vienna graybeards and Saunders at Princeton (idiot), but I am not misled. His methods are flawed, his conclusions unsupported by a shred of reliable evidence -- and yet the plaudits, the laurels, are his and his alone! That his dance language might be accepted (however temporarily) galls me. Sooner someone destroy my own hives, my tapes, my notes, than see his pseudo-science adopted as doctrine.

The scientific community is often impugned by the public it serves for making of skepticism a religion, but in this case a little attention to creed might have been in order. His eloquence and passion for honors has conquered the better judgment of reasonable men, unprepared for the onslaught of Von Slipp's fierce [*The word Kneissl uses is grell, which is more commonly a quality of light, harsh, dazzling. ed.*] ambition. The ridiculous photographs of himself he provides the scientific journals to accompany his papers (what vanity!). His profile, his aspect: every inch the profound and respected biologist. Pah! I've never seen these pictures myself, but I've had them well described to me. Meanwhile my own work in the same area molders in neglectful shade, and I can scarcely afford even the rent on this two room shack in the shadow of the Matterhorn. O Fame! O Fortuna!

"How vainly men themselves amaze," the poet writes [*Quotation in English -- from Marvell. ed.*]. I have a sufficiency of truth unto myself. Watching this buffoon crowned with honors and riches -- as if he were not already an aristocrat! --grows tiresome, and I am tired, too, of writing letters of protest to the appropriate organs.

"Dear Gentlemen of the Academy, it is my sad duty to bring to your attention the following errors...." "Dear Editor, perhaps it would interest your readers to know that you have printed an article containing lies...." "Dear Professor, I warn you for the last time to stop all this nonsense before the Cause Of Science is irreparably harmed...." Never so much the courtesy of a response. I must look a proper fool [*Gimpel, ed.*], a country simpleton [*Einfaltspinsel, ed.*], a stupidhead [*Dummkopf, ed.*]. I, who: struggled from the day I was born; had to educate myself; was not provided with the privilege accorded a high-born like Von Slipp -- I am the one to be scorned? I should be worshipped for my efforts. I have earned my way by the careful husbandry of what small talent God granted me. Unlike some, I was not able to avoid the rigors of military service, nor the unspeakable horror of two wars, by hiding in a research institute.

As a result -- even now I am ashamed to admit -- I am blind as Von Slipp is rich. The hindrance my disability has presented in my work bothers me less than the burden to my daughter, who has in addition to her own troubles the better part of mine to carry on her frail shoulders. She is only sixteen. Because of me the ordinary delights of a young girl are foregone. Because of me, she spends her time attending to an old man's needs instead of attracting a young man's attentions. She is beautiful, and sharp-minded, and graceful in every way, and were she not stuck nursing a cripple in the middle of nowhere suitors would pile up like the drifts of snow under our eaves every fortnight.

We do our best, though. We live. Anna's mother, Hilde, left us when Anna was a baby, not even one year old. Hilde (née Grolsch) had married a reasonably able-bodied university graduate who, before the second war, had a reasonable career as a librarian at the University of Vienna, a fine institution, the oldest University in the German-speaking world, founded in 1365. I worked there happily for twenty years, in the Art and Architecture department, under Dr. Feldman, a wonderful man who went meekly, uncomprehending to the camps and never returned. After the war, everything was different, Vienna no less than my sightless self. I made inquiries at my former office but no one had use for a blind librarian, and I was unwilling to take the position I was offered -- a pathetic sinecure, offered out of pity for a broken war veteran, and hardly enough to support a wife and infant daughter. But I do not blame the University: what else could they do? Likewise I do not blame my wife for leaving: what else could she do? I had returned an invalid, bitter and proud but useless, who had moreover saddled her with a child and no means to feed or clothe her. Anna was conceived during a two-day leave from the Eastern Front in fall of 1944, three months before the grenade blast that robbed me of my eyes.

I was hopeless with guns. In the literal heat of battle -- which is always hot whatever the weather, because the body heats radically in its suit of fear -- huddled at the bottom of a foxhole next to the severed parts of several colleagues, it was much more than I could do to stop my hands shaking long enough to bolt my rifle, which moreover was clotted with mud and ice and grease. Even had I mastered myself sufficiently to climb to the top of my hole and try to shoot, nothing but vague images, shadows, running through the artillery smog, would present themselves as targets. I will tell you now that I shot only once in my military career, and that in so doing I murdered the woolen hat of my sergeant which he had lost leaping into a nearby defilade. By the time the war was over, in May, and I had returned home, guided by a fourteen-year-old Wehrmacht recruit, my wife had remaining less than one month of confinement before giving birth, in late May, to the daughter I have never seen but whose existence has been my only joy. Before the end of the year Hilde was gone, moved back to her mother's in Salzburg and remarried within two years' time to a bricklayer, who naturally prospered in the postwar reconstruction.

Had begun keeping bees before being called away to the war, and when I returned and could not find any real work, the bees were our salvation. Soon learned the layout of my backyard's rows of hives, and could navigate without help their orderly ranks. When she was old enough, little Anna helped carry the dripping combs to the little shack where we scraped them into pans, and then filtered the raw honey into mason jars. I hired a housekeeper when I could afford one, but for the most part we made do for ourselves. I learned to judge locations from intensities of sound. I learned the pattern of echoes from familiar objects, and developed such familiarity with their unseen outlines that I imagined, in my inky cave, that I could see the shadows on the wall, so to speak. At night I had vividly-colored dreams -- my oneiric life was bright, well-sighted, visionary in the truest sense. I often woke up crying.

What is the language of bees? I know, and you know, Anna, my only daughter, my love. We know. The bees speak to you, and you alone understand their honeyed tongue. We discovered your gift by accident, years ago -- you could not have been more than nine -- when you chased a little blue butterfly in the clover between the rows of my hives while I checked the humming honeycombs. Accidentally you knocked into the leg supporting one of the hives and the whole construction toppled over, perilously close to where you frolicked. I could not see this happen, of course; but my memory of the event, stitched together from the evidence of my remaining senses and your own account, has stayed with me as if I had. I shouted an alarm: but you turned and faced the gathering swarm, and spoke several inhuman syllables in a sweet, singing tone that had an immediate calming effect on the bees, who regrouped and returned to their damaged hive -- which I rushed to set right upon receiving assurance that you were unharmed.

"Papa, the bees are sad," you said to me.

"I know, sweetheart, but we will make them happy again soon. Their house is broken but we will fix it for them. I'm only glad they did not choose to sting you."

"Oh, but I told them I was sorry."

"That was surely the right thing to do. But the bees don't speak our language, so they may not have understood you."

"That's why I used their language, Papa. At first they were angry about the damage to their hive but when I explained that it was an accident and that I was only trying to catch the little butterfly, they laughed and warned me to be more careful."

Naturally I ascribed Anna's story to the invention of a precocious child. Naturally I treated her with the benign condescension of all good parents everywhere. I asked her how she had learned the bees' language, when no one else had even thought the bees might speak. She replied, sensibly, that she did not know, but that she understood everything the bees said and they seemed to understand her as well. I asked her to demonstrate. She did, to my satisfaction (this process took place over several weeks and months, but I am conflating for effect). When she spoke bee-language, Anna's voice took on a pure high tone that her regular speaking voice would not seem capable of producing. Indeed, she told me later, when she was older, that the tones were produced largely in her nasal cavities, and that if I could see her when she spoke bee-language I would laugh, because she had to throw her head back and flare her nostrils to get the right sounds.

Convinced that she was neither inventing nor imagining her ability to converse with bees in their own tongue, I resolved to document her gift, and when I had accumulated sufficient evidence to present to the unsuspecting world the irrefutable secrets of the *apis*. Who knew what wisdom lay locked in the many-chambered hive?

Then came Von Slipp, with his dancing bees, who direct their colleagues to fruitful pollen sites and back by means of a complex system of wagging and wiggling. He has published articles and books detailing the experiments he has conducted to prove his ideas. Anna has read me these books and articles, and described to me these ludicrous diagrams. She has related to me the derision of the bees themselves when told about Von Slipp's crackpot notions. "Figwort-head" he is called in their language, which is bee-slang for fat-faced and stupid, Anna tells me. But the immediate acceptance by the scientific community of Von Slipp's ideas doomed my own efforts to present the true bee-language with any degree of credulity. I had not his credentials, his connections, his eloquence. I was the crackpot, not he. I dictated letters, I dictated articles, and now I dictate this journal, although no longer to my daughter Anna, sweet amanuensis, *qui a disparue* [*thus in French in the MS. ed.*]

Now I tell my tales to the recording machine, as I once recorded the secrets they vouchsafed to you, on spinning reels of magnetic tape, and while you slept in the other room, analyzed the patterns buried in the bees' true words. Because the bees do not speak in plain language, but in cryptic phrases that appear nonsensical to those untrained in the apian way. I think that here my blindness made me an advantage: the loss of one sense sharpens the others, it's said -- and truly so. In the phrases Anna spoke into my tape recording device I heard memes of sense, whole threads of meaning, which were left to me to unspool and rewind according to the dictates of reason.

Where I have failed, I alone am to blame. Where succeeded, God [manuscript breaks off].

6. p. 518 Helpless

The pale of settlement. Things that burn (list). Engine of combustion: life. Correspondence. Repetition. Duplication. The light that draws the flower draws you, too.

The Reluctant King

Alfred the Coward stepped carefully down the shoe-worn steps in front of the library. Shallow grooves in the stone from the treading of shoes, countless, over years and years of students walking to and fro. Even a stone can be worn down, he thought, even marble or in this case granite from a quarry in somewhere in.

He carried two books under his arm and headed across the grass for the shade of an elm tree. *Fraxinus Americana*, Alfred read on the brass plate affixed to the tree's broad trunk. *American Elm*. Not many of these left, I suppose, he thought. Wasted by disease, the beetle who carried the disease from tree to tree or anyway, a bug of some kind. Dutch elm the disease was called, but killed American elms with Dutch efficiency. The men from the city came and chopped down the whole row on our street. The noise from the chainsaws. Like shooting a horse, he thought. No use. Books I'm carrying might have been pulped from that dead wood. Still no use.

He sat down in the shade. The new day was warm and moist, and the morning sun had just risen above the slate rooftop of the library. The lowest branches of the elm filtered some of the sunlight through a network of summer leaves, and their complex shadow swayed in the light wind.

Alfred opened one of the books and flipped through the first few chapters without interest. Wonder will the rain hold off until evening, he thought. Right now doesn't look, but these storms move quickly. Two nights ago came out of nowhere, over the blue hills I can see from my north-facing window, so out of the north. Unusual because most weather travels west to east. Part of the trouble with the world, he thought. Underneath right now the root system absorbs groundwater from the soaked-in rain, dredges the water back up through the trunk to the branches. The leaves need rain for strength, but also sun for photosynthesis. Producing air. Birds sitting on the branches, fluttering, chirping. Never know the names of birds. These are sparrows maybe because most birds you see are sparrows. Sarah said.

She would not come tonight, again, he thought. Only when I don't expect. Some trick to that. Some extra sense. Nothing happens except when I'm not looking. He picked a small stone out of the earth at the base of the tree. The stone was round and smooth, with an irregularity, a small dark spot, on the underside. The top of the stone was lighter than the bottom, bleached by the sun. Alfred fingered the stone. Cool to the touch and absurdly smooth, he thought. Worn by rain same as the steps were worn by human feet.

He tossed the stone a little distance. A bird flew down from the tree to inspect the stone. Thinks it might be food, he thought. All day long looking for food, then sleep. I have so much trouble sleeping. No need to look for food, just go the dining hall and heaps of food in steaming piles on my plate. Tonight maybe chicken and a bit of salad for balance. The bird looks for food and I eat the bird. Not this bird. Still, a hawk might, if hawks are here. Never seen one, floating in the currents like on television. Everyone is prey. I don't remember a single prayer, thought Alfred. Haven't been inside a church in years.

A figure approached Alfred across the grass. Looks like Robert, tall and thin with shirttails flapping as he walks, he thought. Like the hanger's still in his shirt, bony shoulders, narrow neck.

Aren't you going for breakfast? asked Robert, stopping a few feet from where Alfred sat.

Alfred gestured to his books. Need to get some reading done. Class at eleven.

Nothing like leaving things to the last minute. Robert reached one bony hand to the back of his neck, scratched lightly.

Better late than never.

O that's clever. I wish I'd thought of that, said Robert.

Alfred squinted up at Robert. Why doesn't he sit down? Makes me nervous looming. Sit down or move on.

What kind of class?

English. We're reading romantic poems, said Alfred. I mean from the period of the Romantics.

Keats died of tuberculosis. Consumption as it was called then. The wasting disease.

Yes that's very helpful. I'll be sure to mention that fact to the professor.

He was only twenty-five or something, said Robert. Not much older than us.

I suppose that's true. Keats was a bell struck once, with a heavy hammer, in the distance, thought Alfred. You hear the fading of the sound rather than the sound itself. But the sound never fades completely. What does echolalia mean? I remember looking it up just the other day.

What does echolalia mean? asked Alfred.

Echolalia, repeated Robert. I don't know. Did you read it somewhere? Echolalia.

No, it just popped into my head. I came across it a few days ago. I think maybe something Sarah said. Obviously it has something to do with echoes.

Obviously.

Robert stood for a moment, silent, in the gathering heat of the day.

I'll leave you to your reading, he said after a while.

Okay. You doing anything later?

Robert shrugged. He held his palms slightly outwards in a gesture of helplessness. No plans. Call me if you think of something.

Maybe, said Alfred. I'll see you. When he held his hands like that he was the picture of Christ. Except for the lack of beard, and also now Jesus was said to be a black man. But pictures of Christ from paintings. Except for the beard. His hair's not dissimilar, though, in length. Also lank and greasy, as you'd expect. A holy man would not take many baths, I think, he thought.

Alfred watched Robert walk towards the dining hall, which sat at a right angle to the library. The dining hall was made of red brick with white wooden columns. Those are Ionic capitals, he thought. Ionic, Doric, Corinthian. Everything I remember from Ancient Greece.

A gust of wind rustled the branches above his head. One or two of the birds flew off. Shading his eyes with his hand, Alfred peered in the direction of the sun. A few thin gray clouds scudded across the sky, moving fast. Down here the wind is calmer, thought Alfred. In the atmosphere things are more turbulent. The air is thinner and colder and changeable. When you fly in a plane you may encounter sudden pockets of rough air and the plane may drop, suddenly, in certain extreme cases hundreds of feet in a second.

He turned back to the book in his lap. The book had nothing to do with Romantic poetry. It was a novel by a French writer from the nineteenth century, translated into English by a fin-de-siècle British lady who had translated many books. Must have become easy after a while, he thought. Don't see how you can produce things in that quantity without falling back on habit. With translation you're always left to wonder if the book is a reflection more of the translator or of the original author.

You don't seem yourself lately, said Alfred.

Sarah stretched across his bed, her hair wet from the shower, dressed in a light-blue blouse and gym shorts.

Who do I seem like, she asked. She was leaning on her elbows, watching the sunset fade outside his window.

I don't know. Not yourself.

Don't know what to say to that. I am myself. How can I not seem like myself? I don't know any other way to be.

No, it's just, you're always sad and you don't want to talk to me about things. You don't get interested the way you used to.

Maybe I've told you everything I'm interested about. Maybe we've used up all possible topics of conversation. Anyway, I don't feel particularly sad. You may be projecting.

Alfred sat at his desk and pretended to work on a paper for a class. He had a few sheets of paper covered in notes, and an open book on the desk in front of him. He held a pencil in his right hand. The pencil was covered in teeth marks.

I don't think so. I mean, I don't think I'm projecting. But it's possible I'm wrong about your mood. I don't have much experience with other people.

That's not true, said Sarah, craning on the bed to face Alfred. You have more experience than you need. You have a surfeit of experience. You have me. You have yourself. By measuring one against the other you can draw any conclusion you need, and you have a fifty-fifty chance of being right. That's better odds than with most things.

I've never had any luck with numbers, said Alfred, turning back to his work.

That was the last time, he thought, sitting under the elm, four days and counting. I try not to notice or let her absence bother me but what else? Alfred dug his fingers into the small hollow left by the stone he had picked out. He loosened clumps of black earth and flicked them with thumb and forefinger into the grass. The clumps disintegrated on impact. Earthworms churn the earth, building tunnels, an endless, unseen lattice. We need the earthworms because they till the soil, turning and turning the compact earth until it loosens and can absorb the rainwater on which all things depend. Once I bit into an apple I'd plucked from one of the trees in the faculty gardens. There was a worm in the apple and I bit it in half. I spit the worm and the piece of apple from my mouth and chucked the rest of the apple into a bush. Some worms can regenerate themselves from even half. Or maybe I killed the worm, I don't know, he thought.

He inspected the nails on the hand that had rummaged in the dirt. There was a thin line of dirt under each nail. He tried to clean the nails with a pencil he had wedged in one of the books as a placeholder. Only makes things worse, he thought.

Alfred returned the pencil to its place in the book. Again he leafed through the book's pages, without reading. This is not the book I wanted, he thought. *Nunc ipsum, tamen.* I will not knuckle under the weight of ideas. I will not say uncle.

The Speed of Things

Part 1: Ego in Arcadia

Nothing would make me happier than to tell you, up front, that everything works out fine in the end. Can't do that, I'm afraid. Not because things don't work out fine in the end, but because I don't know how the end ends. The end hasn't happened yet (as far as I can tell). The end may never happen. Things are moving so quickly these days that the end may come and go and I might not notice. Have to allow for that possibility. Have to allow for every possibility. Facts are engrams. Engrams are hypothetical. Thus: Every. Possible. Outcome.

As for the body lying on the floor a few feet away from where I sit, at my desk: I can talk about that. I can give you a definitive answer with respect to the body. Yes, the blood pooling near her head and, less obviously, the little splatters on and around her bare feet: aftereffects of her transition from life to death by means of a series of bullets discharged from a handgun at close range. I should probably make this much (all right, fine) clear: I did not shoot the gun. She didn't shoot the gun. I have no idea who shot the gun. Not sure it matters. The gun got shot, right? A shot gun is not necessarily a shotgun, would be one conclusion you could draw from the.

Cannot let this incident interfere with my work schedule. I am extremely busy. I'm on seven different deadlines. Which when you think about it, as I am sometimes given to do (think about it), presents a sort of *ironie du sort*. (Now I'm just playing word games.) But serious. The line drawn outside a prison beyond which prisoners were liable to be shot. From that idea to this: How? Is there any sense in which missing a deadline corresponds to going further than allowed and therefore liable to be shot and killed? Perhaps going further than allowed, yes, that much one can grant, but everything after therefore is a damned lie.

En attendant, everything is killing me. Not just the seven different deadlines but the expectations. People who know me, who have made the mistake of not shutting up (for good) the minute we met, have a series of expectations that seem to grow, perversely, in accord with my ability to disappoint each and every one. You have to say "each and every" in that sentence for the rhythm, not the meaning. The meaning can go to hell, along with all the people who expect things from me. I know my limits. I know when I've reached my limits. Hey, guess what? I've reached my limits. I might be, well, actually I am, let's not kid ourselves, he said, of at least superhuman intelligence and—did you see that? Her arm just twitched. That was disconcerting—supernal intuition, but even such a one has limits. I see everything, I understand everything, and this happens at both the conscious and all twelve subconscious levels simultaneously. You'd reasonably expect a man with such abilities to be sotted with power, joy-drunk, unintimidated by intimations of mortality. To some extent that is actual factual. To some extent just silly. I have to draw the. It's a question of. Guess. Guess not. Huh.

In the motion picture *Meet John Doe* starring that one guy and that girl and directed by what's-his-name (1939), movement is both created and just happens. Think on this: w/r/t film and music, all forms of dissemination heretofore have involved circular objects, spinning. No matter how far back you looky-loo. Revolvers each and every one, but no more, no more, no more, no more. I don't "these days" know the shape of the medium. Does anyone? Is there a shape? I have seen certain media represented as a waveform, but I suspect that waveform is merely a visual translation of a shapeless batch of numbers. Thing I need to know, has art become math or has math become art, (and) is there a meaningful distinction?

A John Doe club forms for the purpose of improving relations between and among neighbors. That's all. To be a better neighbor. Not really sure how such a thing, even if fueled by a despicable despot, takes root and flowers. Where I live, there are only seven or ten people grouped in ten or seven tin houses, then nothing interesting for many kilometers. An island afloat in the middle of a great city. Everyone is related either by marriage or blood, and everyone keeps to himself. Family members do not talk to family members. No one talks to anyone. Where I live is spectral silent except for noises made by elements and animals. Where I live is nowhere.

The potential when you harness the separate units of a great number of John Doe clubs towards some end other than neighborly. In and out of doors. Well, that's just frightening. If you agree raise your hand. No, other hand. Theoretically I am writing a history of the Federal Reserve Bank. I say theoretically because I don't believe the Federal Reserve Bank exists, evidence to the contrary notwithstanding. You could I suppose say with some accuracy that I'm writing a history of nothing. The History of Nothing. Written in Nowhere. Written By. (Hope is in the hand that hits you.)

I have been contracted. Contacted? After a while you forget the smaller differences. This is a known side effect, according to the materials accompanying my prescription of Provigil. I thank, I praise, I grant every, no, each and every day. One hundred milligrams in the morning is my prescriptive dose. I'm not good at following instructions. Too proud or something. Nine is the number of the muses, so nine hundred milligrams in the morning suits my symmetry. Many people say: "Where would I be without coffee" and for coffee you can substitute other stimulants or depressants or ampersands. But where would I be without coffee? Added to nine muses of Provigil you can accomplish worlds. You can eliminate sleep from your diet. How super my love!

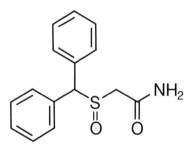

C15H15NO2S

Walking through tall pines, trunks pasted with greeny moss, forest floor covered in Mass of needles and cones and deciduous leaves, brown or yellow according to their last request, Aunt Panne was over-brimmed with holy spirit of trees. Praying as she walked, slowly, for soul of dead girl lying on the floor next to desk of Writer. Dead girl or possibly not-dead girl, *id est* dying girl. Lovely deep blue of her lips.

Mossy ruins of a water mill. Heavy-set old man with dropsical jowls and comically large glasses sat on a rotting tree limb chewing a reed.

"I am Aunt Panne."

"I am Paul Volcker, twelfth Chairman of the Federal Reserve, 1979-1987. I grew up in Teaneck, New Jersey."

"What brings you to the forest, Paul Volcker?"

"I'm waiting for Writer to remember me."

"There's a plaque here by the ruin of the millstone. I can't read it."

"Because it's in Gallic. The gist of the inscription is that these ruins are symbolic of a larger wreck."

"Well, that makes sense. Did you know the dead or dying girl?"

"Not personally. Only what you read in papers. When there used to be papers. Newspapers, I mean. *Les journaux.*"

"It wasn't all that long ago."

"No, it wasn't. You're right."

"By larger wreck you mean the design?"

"Yes."

"I've been wondering lately if the seeming incoherence of the design isn't contained, somehow, within an even larger design whose outlines we can't see. And that maybe this imperceptible scheme makes perfect sense."

"I don't engage with poetry." Paul Volcker stopped chewing his reed and fished in his jacket pocket for a small notebook.

"*Meet John Doe,*" he read aloud from the notebook.

"And then what?" asked Aunt Panne.

"That's all I have so far."

"It's a good start."

Aunt Panne left Paul Volcker sitting by the remains of the mill and continued through the forest, following a path that was no path. She knew that Paul Volcker was worried about the farmers driving their tractors down C Street NW to blockade the Eccles Building, but he would never admit it, not to her, anyway. Maybe he wouldn't admit it to anyone, anymore. Maybe the reason he wouldn't admit it is related to the reason he was sitting on the rotting tree limb by the old water mill.

Was there even a trace of whatever water source once drove the mill? As she moved farther and farther away, Aunt Panne's memory similarly receded. She could no longer picture Paul Volcker's face. She could no longer in any detail picture the mossy ruin of the mill. It was entirely possible, she admitted to herself as she trudged up a gentle slope slick with mud from a recent rain, that she had imagined the whole interval. The words *lacuna* and *caesura* flitted through her brain for a moment, and then disappeared.

Okay, but if you allow one example do you have to allow them all? Do you admit the unreality of experience generally if one experience turns out to be illusion? The brain is capable of many things when its circuits are working, even more when overloaded with catecholamines and hypothalamic histamines. The synaptic terminals release these oracles into the floodstream and you start to see things: Is it the future? Is it the past? Is it a kind of present that would otherwise be invisible to our seven dulled senses? Or is it, as most would have you think, a fantasy, product of a disordered mind. Consciousness infected with chemicals, perception out of step with consensus. When you apply reason to the problem, you kill the problem. You derive a solution. Aunt Panne mistrusted solutions. She would rather beggar the question by withholding logic, and thus arrive at the edge of the forest rather than, say, a small clearing or a mossy ruin.

Approaching the ecotone she could see cows grazing in the meadow.

Part 2: Rule Bretagne
* * *

Snow came in bunches to Bon Repos, on the border of the Forêt de Quénécan. The companions of the Abbey were put to work sweeping the courtyard early on the morning of December 19 in the Year of Our Lord. The blinking lights of the snowplows had moved far enough away from the courtyard that you could no longer hear the susurrus of their heavy tires, nor the scrape of metal against. This has been the coldest winter of our lives. In the memory of our lives. There has been a record chute of snow. The cars are corked for miles, and hours, on the autoroutes. On the radio you are warned to bring a thermos of some hot liquid and "perhaps something to eat" before you set out in your car. What kind of a person would set out in his car under such perturburant circumstances? What kind of person says "set out in his car"? The wrecked bulkheads massed along the shore, covered in fresh snow, no longer move, but boy they sure do work. How do you cut the GPS tag from under your skin? You use a stolen knife. You ask the girl to use the knife because you can't do it yourself. That's how the girl ended up dead, on your floor, in your room, because she removed the GPS tag. It's starting to come back now, but in fragments. In packets.

Everybody's got a past. Everybody stinks of time. But the photography is so pure that you don't mind. The rhythm of the shots, and the rhythm within the shots, match with exquisite rigor the languid movements of the actors inside the frame. Only the music jars. The music is ridiculous, overstated, too much. "Tonight the gates of Mercy will open." That's what the music wants to say. The clarinets. I see a crowd of black hats, everyone playing the clarinet. There's nothing wrong with the clarinet in principal. With any woodwind.

New rule: No one speaks. Not for any reason. Words have only ever caused problems. I can think of no exceptions. Everything will be communicated in images, only. No intertitles, subtitles, supertitles, titles, title cards. The moving image versus the static (photo) is obviously superior. An image that moves offers a more complete set of the infinite fractions of solitude, according to N. The history of cinema is the history of the image. Without words. The paradox of using words to describe things that. Text is text is text. This is not a text. In the event of an actual text, you would have been directed by the appropriate emergency services to destroy all evidence of yourself. I do not feel pain. Thunder and lightning ask my approval. What some call prayer is easily misused, but I command the seas.

I have no reason to doubt. I have no reason to believe. I got no reason, I prefer no reason at all. Crows gather on every street corner. Talking about something I can't quite. What's the point of so many crows? Crown, crow, cow. Unusually, you can do that in Russian, too.

Phil Esposito was the consensus pick in the living room for the trivia question "Which Buckthorn had been the fastest to score fifty goals in one season." Writer didn't wait to hear the answer. If not Esposito, who? Cashman? Bucyk? What difference does it make? They were all fucking great. Ten seconds later his father actually said: "I have seen some terrible calls in my life, but that one takes the cake," concerning a potentially dodgy hooking call on Buckthorn player Sad Strawbo. The answer to a more pertinent question was soon thereafter provided by Sabater Pi and his caliginous table of incantatory engrams. Without the help of Sabater Pi, one finds it unlikely that anything would ever get done by anyone. A study of helicopter pilots suggested that 600 mg of Provigil given in three doses can be used to keep pilots alert and maintain their accuracy at pre-deprivation levels for 40 hours without sleep. Another study of fighter pilots showed that Provigil given in three divided 100 mg doses sustained the flight control accuracy of sleep-deprived F-117 pilots to within about 27 percent of baseline levels for 37 hours, without any considerable side effects.

The exact mechanism of action of Provigil is unclear, although numerous studies have shown it to increase the levels of various monoamines, namely: dopamine in the striatum and nucleus accumbens; noradrenaline in the hypothalamus and ventrolateral preoptic nucleus; and serotonin in the amygdala and frontal cortex. While the co-administration of a dopamine antagonist is known to decrease the stimulant effect of amphetamine, it does not entirely negate the wakefulness-promoting actions of Provigil. This is not by any means the whole story. Sabater Pi stands over his engrams and mutters incantations. These incantations are the stuff of ice creams, through which the world learns its manners. Without Sabater Pi's engrams, the world would have no memory. He decides which to keep and which to discard. It's a very important job. It might be the only important job. Sabater Pi had just decided that the engram of the dead girl in Writer's room must at all costs be kept. Could not for any reason be removed. He walked to a corner of his office, sat down at a comically small desk, and began typing.

Writer was startled by the sudden whir and clunk of the fax machine on the floor by his feet. He remembered that the Icelandic magician Flute Guðmundsdottir had once told him that her magic was meant to represent or emulate the sound of the modern world, its electronic machinery in constant motion, humming and buzzing and belling in the background even when no one was listening. This had never made any sense to Writer. He had tried to discuss the issue with Bragi Ólafsson, an Icelandic novelist who had once helped out in Sykurmolarnir, which was the name of a circus act in which Flute had also participated, doing—something. But Writer's attempt to reach Ólafsson through his American publisher had been unsuccessful, and so with some reluctance he had dropped the matter. Throughout his conversation with Flute, she had licked her lips repeatedly, small pink tongue darting out of her mouth to moisten this or that small section of un-glossed upper or lower lip. It was a reflexive action. She wasn't aware she was doing that, he remembered thinking. But also a familiar one. People who are nervous, or who take any form of stimulant, even coffee, are prone to this reflex. The stimulant produces a sensation of dryness in the mouth and lips that no amount of water can remedy. There would be no reason, Writer reasoned, for Flute to be nervous in his company, in Room 59 of the Chateau Marmont in Los Angeles, California. She was drinking from a deep glass of still water. It was exactly noon o'clock.

The sound of the modern world scared the wits right out of Writer (whose real name was Thomas Early). The sound of the modern world was linked inextricably to the speed of the modern world. The latter was very, very fast, and getting faster. At—what's the usual phrase—an "exponential rate". One moment we're all prosperous and happy, seals basking on the warm rocks of midday sun off the coast of Maine in summer. The next we're falling endlessly down a hole that had been a floor but was no longer a floor. The banking system had run out of money, as Thomas Early understood the situation, and so everyone had run out of money, and even though everyone had run out of money years and years ago, for some reason this now actually mattered. Hence the panicky tumble down the black hole of the future, end over end, bottom over top, will-ye nill-ye, and God help us if we ever reach any kind of definite denouement, because a back-of-the-envelope calculation indicates that an abrupt halt would result in a gelatinous mess.

The best we can hope for, then, in the current situation, is to keep falling. Even though it seems as if we're falling faster and faster, we're actually falling at the same speed. The speed of a falling object does not depend on its mass. That you are a (much) fatter person than me does not mean you will fall faster. We all started at the same height, from the same point, and Galileo has proved that we will all be crushed to death simultaneously.

* * *

We are aware of our many misdeeds, our failings, our weaknesses, our fears, our shame. We do not know how to exculpate ourselves. (Having no religion to rely on.) We do not know whether to exculpate ourselves, having no moral or philosophical base from which to extrude the principle of sin. Because we were brought up short. We were all brought up short in a long, tall world.

The dead girl's mistake was indulging her appetite for existence. We all make the same mistake, and the mistake is always fatal. An eighty-three year old woman is in a coma after having been attacked at the métro Mairie-de-Clichy (Hauts-de-Seine) by a fourteen year old Romanian kid. A former journalist was killed by his seventeen year old son because the son was unhappy with the five hundred euros per month his father was giving him as an allowance. A man found two thousand euros, cash, in the street. He turned it over to the police. A judge ruled that the two thousand euros does not belong to the man, and is instead being kept by the court until the real owner of the money can be determined. The man declared himself in an interview to be "disappointed" by the court's ruling. "Honesty doesn't pay," he said.

Potter's Field ain't such a faraway stare when you've one foot in the quick. An argument between scholars, already tenuous, becomes untenably ephemeral within minutes if you put it in (a cloud). Unsearchable, unfindable, irretrievable. Lost. The most common side effect of speed is the acceleration of loss.

The fax from Sabater Pi was very short. It read, in full: "The dead or dying girl is you."

Elephants

The elephants were buried in sand up to their necks. From a certain distance, all you could see were dozens of trunks, waving like sea grass in the desert air, and enormous floppy ears. The elephants repeatedly slapped their ears on the ground, sending vibrations through the sand that would return, with news, upon encountering solid objects. A rock, for instance. Or a truck carrying boxes of protesting chickens. Or a Bradley Light Armor vehicle. In this way the elephants could gauge proximity of danger.

You dream of a thing like this. You don't ask for it but you dream. Also you eat, you sleep, you walk in a seeming trance through the maze of daily tasks that make up a life. Then you notice there are elephants buried up to their necks in the sand half a mile off the interstate. Maybe the elephants have always been there. Maybe they didn't exist until you noticed them. Maybe they don't exist. Maybe you don't. The elephants make you wonder where before you didn't wonder.

These are not stupid elephants. They are smart, well-trained, and have constructed, mostly with their trunks—which are more flexible than any human arm, and which can cradle a baby or rip a tree from the ground by its roots—a series of deep trenches in the shifty earth to protect them from our wrath.

Elephants won a war for Hannibal. He crossed the Alps at winter, when the best military thinking declared the Alps impassable due to drifting snow and mistral wind. The elephants, though at times buried to their necks in snowdrift, were able to lumber unstoppably both up and down the treacherous alpine passes, carrying troops armed with spears. Not a few elephants, you'd imagine, tumbled into icy chasms and died. Hannibal didn't stop.

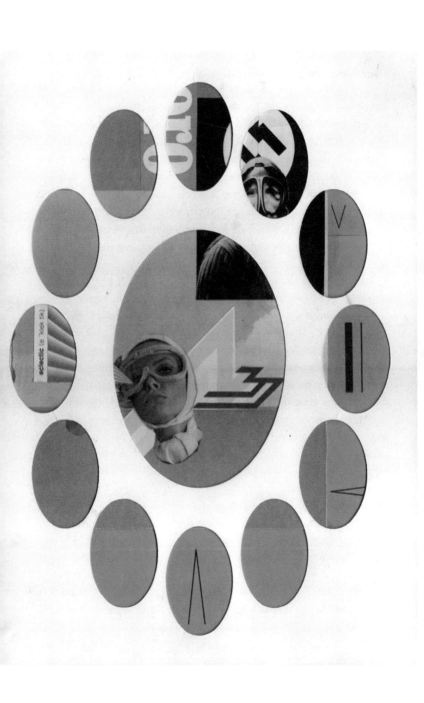

The Hill of Crosses

I wake early on the morning of September 14th. There is something strange about the shadows in the little chapel so I go outside to check. From a narrow rise just behind the grouping of lime trees you can see down into the Cassentino, and I stand and watch the ripples of wind in the moonlit grass, in the glittery lake. Yes, the moon is full, or nearly. Its position in the sky is such that when I turn back to see the chapel, the stone is bright, almost glowing.

There are voices in the trees. There are always voices in the trees. Even when the wind is still, even when the birds sleep, I hear voices. What I would like to do is throw a pebble all the way from here into the valley. It is 1,283 meters below me. It is the year 1224. These numbers cannot be coincidence. I have just under 1,300 friends on Facebook. Again: really?

I sit down on the narrow rise, between two half-buried granite slabs. It's possible that this is a burial mound, from ages ago. That bones lie under my bones. And anyway rocks are a kind of bones, too, the bones of earth, of tiny creatures and plants rotted and pressed together by a force greater than gravity. I mean that you need time, of course. Without time gravity is just a magic trick.

The strangeness in the shadows, I see now, is a quality of light. The moon is ringed by something blue, maybe just a cloud, maybe a premonition of apocalypse. Maybe both. My problem is, I can never make up my mind. That's why it has to be just me, here, by myself, in the little chapel. I mean except for you, Leo. It's okay you're here, although to be honest, I wish you wouldn't follow me around everywhere.

Not bothered about not eating these past twenty-odd days, no, but I would kill for a cigarette. And a goddamn cup of coffee. That's the hardest thing about fasting: it's not the nourishment but the rituals you miss. The little habits that knit the separate parts of the day into wearable cloth. Praying is great, I'm all for prayer, and the regular intervals certainly impose a kind of rigor, but. A little formal for my taste. I'm a casual guy. I like to think of myself as spontaneous. For instance: I just farted. I didn't have to tell you. Maybe you wouldn't even notice, or maybe you would but you're too polite to say anything. But I don't care. I farted. That's me.

So here we are, sitting on the narrow rise between two half-buried granite slabs, or boulders, or the ossified shoulders of giants...

Did you see that? No, of course you didn't, you never see anything. You're too busy smelling my farts.

I... what? Wait! Shit. O holy shit. Fucking bloody hell!

Look, Leo, look: in the center of each palm. And it... well, it... fuck! Yes, it hurts, I mean, what the hell? All of a sudden there was this seraph, this six-winged angel on a cross, floating right in front of me...

And you saw nothing. Are you messing with my head right now, because I really don't. Okay. Well, then she... *announces* in a voice as loud as any bell, but that apparently rang only inside my head, since you obviously didn't hear anything... right? Okay. She *proclaims* that she's giving me the five wounds of Christ. That's an almost exact quote. The five wounds of Christ. So, look, I've got these bleeding palms, and also these bleeding feet, and the one that really sucks, this one in my chest where the Roman soldier pierced him with a spear

Yes, Leo, I am in a bad fucking mood. Who wouldn't be? What kind of gift is this? First of all, it hurts like hell, like I said. Second of all, now I'm only going to live four more years. And then what? Sainthood? What good is Sainthood? I'd rather have a cup of coffee and a goddamn cigarette.

Tell you what, Leo, I could rip your fucking throat out without a second thought. I am the gentlest soul on earth and still I would rip your throat fucking out. Because that's the flip side, Jack Christ, that's the hidey-hole where he keeps his secrets, and I have the key, because he gave me the key when he. And no harm shall come to the little ones. A promise is a promise, buddy, and I don't care who your father is or what strings he can pull, you do not break a promise to a child. You get me, man? Stop staring at the wounds, what's the matter, you've never seen a man bleed slowly to death over a period of years by supernaturally-inflicted wounds before? Lighten up, Leo. You're bringing me down. I don't need weeping and rending of garments right now. I need a level head. I need some bandages, to be honest. You think you can manage to get me some bandages? That'd be great.

In a few hundred years, long after I'm dead, they'll start

placing crosses on a hill in Lithuania. Even after the communists come and periodically wipe the place clean, the crosses will return. Not just crosses, either, but giant crucifixes, carvings, statues of the Virgin, hundreds of tiny effigies and rosaries and icons. Over a hundred thousand crosses by the year 2010. And a few years before that they'll build a little hermitage nearby. Its interior decoration will draw links with this place, because the brothers that build the chapel will call themselves Franciscans, after me. Because supposedly they're following my work. I mean, maybe they are. That would be nice. That would mean something, I guess. It's too bad we won't live to see that, huh, Leo? Lithuania. That's a long way away.

Liberty, Or Something.

Oscar Delacroix, no relation,—sitting in Les Grandes Marches under L'Opéra Bastille with a good view of the bustling Place, and its central figure (Liberty, or something)—is barely present. She stops writing, puts down her pen. Takes one lump of *sucre roux* from the saucer and drops it into her espresso. Picks up a spoon and stirs, gently. She never looks to see if the lump (le morceau) hits or misses the cup, which is after all not large, nor does she bother to determine with her spoon whether the lump (le morceau) has dissolved completely before raising the cup to her lips and taking a sip.

Oscar has been making a list in her notebook of the things that break her heart: 1) Girl in pleated, dark-blue skirt who removes her glasses with left hand, carelessly, slips one temple in her shirt pocket, turns from a bookstore window to greet a friend. She was looking at Pinget's *Mahu*, which (typically) did not look back. Books are too proud. No wonder no one reads. 2) The undertow of melancholy that tugs at her stomach when the light is low and slanted through Porte Saint-Denis and couples drink on *gaslit terrasses*. 3) How dust motes and dust mites denote two very different things: the former unspeakably lovely, the latter ugly and pathogenic. Separated, forever, by a typo. How a lovely night for mothing became a lovely night for nothing, in *The Gift* by Nabokov, unless that's a beautiful myth. 4) A yellow coincidence, hovering on her windowsill at daybreak. 5) The number five.

Oscar is currently preoccupied with a story told to her late last night in Café Flore by a friend, the American poet George Allen Parker, who is in Paris studying at the Sorbonne—she can't remember what, exactly, because even if George Allen Parker is studying the most fascinating subject ever taught, he is still only studying. So for now he is not the American poet George Allen Parker but the American student George Allen Parker.

George Allen Parker told Oscar a story about a young musician, relatively successful (!), relatively well-known (!!), who decided one night, here in Paris (!!!) to drop acid and take a motorcycle ride. Which ended, as most things do, against a wall on the Rue du Nil (9e arrondissement), which is less a "rue" and more a "ruelle," but which nonetheless ends abruptly in a brick wall. The guy, the musician, survived, but his looks and career were ruined. He spent several months in the hospital and when discharged remained in Paris, in the care of his mother who had flown there to be with her son and who now rents a small apartment near Père Lachaise. Metro Phillippe Auguste (Blue Line, No. 2, near the border of the 11e and 20e arrondissements, opened 31 January, 1903). The former musician rarely goes out in public, but you can occasionally see him walking near the Musée des arts et métiers, which is his favorite museum, though he never goes inside.

He's become a painter. He paints his dreams, which are all oneiric distortions of his accident. The American student George Allen Parker claims that the former musician/accident victim/painter is plagued by headaches so severe that he requires two or three months a year of further hospitalization, and that the only way he has been able to manage the pain with any success is through painting. Well, painting and morphine.

It is no longer legal to smoke indoors in Paris cafés or restaurants, but Oscar withdraws a cigarette from a pack of Gauloises Blondes (Red) and lights it with a wooden match. No one seems to notice. No one bothers her. The story the American student George Allen Parker told her was clearly a fabrication, but she can't figure out why he would invent something so pointless in such detail, down to Metro stop and favorite museum and so on.

Exhaling a blue plume of smoke that spirals to the ceiling of Les Grandes Marches, she suddenly remembers that George Allen Parker is studying anthropology at the Sorbonne. Of course: the science of cartoons. Everything makes sense now, including the girl in front of the bookstore, maybe especially the girl in front of the bookstore.

Now that she thinks of it, Oscar isn't even sure that the drug-addled motorcyclist in George Allen Parker's story was male. For some reason, the details have already started to withdraw from her memory's outstretched arms into the kind of dense fog one normally associates with London, but which in fact occurs in Paris regularly, though not as regularly as one might wish. In fact, this fog can happen anywhere, though no cases have been reported for many years in Valdux, South Dakota.

Kuznetsova, Cibulkova, Schiavone, counted Oscar, practicing

her Spanish for an upcoming interview with the great Ecuadorian writer Charles Panic. He's lived in Paris for ten years, but you can never be sure that a foreigner here speaks French. Oscar knows many people who've lived in Paris close to ten years and never bothered to learn French, because you don't really need to, so long as you can speak English. Every Parisian speaks English, without exception, even if he won't admit it. The American novelist Daniel Daniels, for instance: he's been here forever with his Romanian boyfriend and neither of them speak a word of French. Oscar suspects that Daniels understands a lot more than he lets on, and is only unwilling to speak the language because he finds his accent ugly, which makes him self-conscious.

Oscar looks down at the notebook lying by her left hand, opens it and flips through a few pages, left- and off-handedly. A quote from Cocteau: *one should cultivate that for which others criticize you most: that's the most original part of you, your essence.* W. W. was a real painter, even if she only painted aquarelles. Her art was on book covers. Her art had been mass-produced. A real artist is always reproduced, in order to make him accessible to the Other.

Nonetheless, Oscar thinks that present accessibility as a measure of enduring worth is worthless, because there are so many truly awful artifacts (from an aesthetic standpoint) that are widely accessible, even widely praised: for example that new book by Augustus Franz — another American! — the name is on the tip of her tongue… *Liberty, or something.* Maybe it's exactly that: Liberty, Or Something. Middlebrow trash, but the critics cling like iron filings to this, this, this magnetic nonsense.

Even the American student George Allen Parker's motorcycle story is better than *Liberty, Or Something*, which is a fat, sleek book, like a seal lying on the rocks, sunbathing at midday, occasionally barking something meaningless to an audience of awed spectators (those close enough to see the seal, some of whom have perhaps never seen a seal), who naturally find the seal enchanting, and read into the barks (which are really quite ugly, and could only appeal to a tin-eared person) fireworks of meaning where there exists, in fact, not even a damp squib.

Such, sighed Oscar, such, such. She motioned to the waiter for the check, but there was no waiter. No table, no notebook, no restaurant, no Place de la Bastille. No such person as the American student George Allen Parker. No such person, Oscar reminded herself, as Oscar Delacroix (no relation). Only a body swathed head-to-toe in bandages at the Hôpital Americain de Paris, 63 Boulevard Victor Hugo, Neuilly-sur-Seine, which is hardly even Paris, it's so far north and west of the city center. The authorities (Who are the authorities? thought Oscar. Are you the authorities?) have thus far been unable to identify the body, and the woman who sits in the room with the body refuses to speak, and has not stopped crying for three days. Oscar knows because although swathed in bandages from head to toe, she can still hear, with painful acuity, that some hospital employees believe there is no body underneath the bandages.

Oscar is starting to suspect they may be right. A new left-handed entry to the list of things that break her heart: 6) A misprint on page 113 of the Alan Russell translation of *Madame Bovary*: "life a leaf" instead of "like a leaf". Is that what's meant by poetic justice? She turns her imaginary head to the woman by the side of the bed. All my favorite writers are dead, Mom, and I had no business being on that motorcycle. No business at all.

The Rose Encyclopedia

When Tobias Hume woke the morning of November 12, 1642 at the Charterhouse, a former priory lying just to the north and east of the ancient wall of the City of London, he did not know that he was going to spend the rest of that day writing an essay. Much less that he would later have that essay printed as a pamphlet at his own expense by John Windet, the same who had been entrusted with the manuscript of *Musicall Humors* in 1605, or to give the full title: *The First Part of Ayres, French, Pollish, and others together, some in Tablature, and some in Pricke-Song...With Pavines, Galliards, and Almaines for the Viole De Gambo alone, and other Musicall Conceites for two Base Viols, expressing five partes, with pleasant reportes one from the other and for two Leero Viols, and also for the Leero Viole with two Treble Viols or two with one Treble. Lastly for the Leero Viole to play alone, and some Songes to be sung to the Viole, with the Lute, or better with the Viole alone Also an Invention for two to play upon one Viole. Composed by Tobias Hume, Gentleman. London, Printed by John WIndet, dwelling at the Signe of the Crosse Keyes at Powles Wharfe. 1605* .

Nevertheless, Captain Hume found himself back in his room after a spare breakfast infected with a pestilent itch to express his thoughts in writing. He had, during his stay at the Charterhouse, beginning in 1629, been sensible of this itch only twice before: the first time resulted in a petition to Charles I asking for permission to deliver some letters on behalf of the King Of Sweden. In the petition he also requested 120 men to ensure the safe conduct of said letters. He received no reply.

A second itch some five years later was satisfied by a broader entreaty, addressed to the whole of Parliament, entitled *True Petition of Colonel Hume, as it was presented to the Lords assembled in the high Court of Parliament* (the reader will note that Captain Hume has here conferred upon himself a higher rank), and asks that he be given command over the troops sent to Ireland to crush the Catholic rebellion. The petition itself shows some evidence of a disordered mind, ranging from flattery to self-pity. An illustrative excerpt: *I do humbly intreat to know why your Lordships do slight me, as if I were a fool or an Ass...I have pawned all my best clothes, and have now no good garment to wear...I have not one penny to help me at this time to buy me bread, so that I am like to be starved for want of meat and drink, and did walk into the fields lately to gather Snails in the netles, and brought a bag of them home to eat, and do now feed on them for want of other meat, to the great shame of this land and those that do not help me...*

Lest this brief account tumble headlong like a blind sheep over the cliff of Story and onto the rocks of Pathos, it should be noted that at the time, Captain Hume was past the age of sixty, and had made his living for the most part as a professional soldier, serving in the Swedish and Russian armies in their various disputes with Poland, Finland, and each other. His skill in battle, and his long service, were therefore not in dispute, and the fact that he had been relegated to the Charterhouse, which provided shelter for "distressed gentlemen," most of them former officers of the army or navy, artists, and men of letters, proves only that valor on the field of battle was no guarantor of future security in the age of Shakespeare.

In Hume's own words, though, *"My Profession being, as my Education hath beene, Armes, the onely effeminate part of me, hath beene Musicke; which in mee hath beene always Generous, because never Mercenarie."* Thus he is best remembered today not for his military prowess, but for his two published works for viols (including many solo works for the lyra viol) and original songs. The first, referenced earlier, was followed in two years' time by Captain Humes Poeticall Musicke. This at a time when England's dominant instrument was the lute, making Hume's insistence on the superiority of the viol controversial. He was well-known in the early 1600s for bursting into public performances at which the lute was featured and bowing away at his viol with a ferocity and volume that quite overwhelmed both lutist and audience. By the time of his death in 1645, Hume's long campaign on behalf of the viol had achieved its primary goal; the lute had fallen out of fashion, never to be revived, except by the occasional pretentious pop musician attempting to establish his folk bona fides. (See: "Sting," né Gordon Sumner. Or rather, don't see, nor listen.) Sadly, Captain Hume was altogether unaware of his success.

But we digress. With excellent reason, but still. Tobias Hume on the morning of November 12, 1642, had neither music nor warfare on his mind, but Philosophy. Hume was worn out. Profoundly so, to the core of his soul. He was unsure of the cause, but sure that he was not alone in his affliction, and thus as certainly as first principles are based on an intuition of true understanding, he proceeded to the idea that an essay exploring the various types of exhaustion, and offering cures, might prove instructive both for himself and his fellow gentlemen. Two problems presented themselves to him immediately: the first, that he had never received much of an education, and was only as fluent in Latin as any other non-scholarly gentleman, and therefore would have to write in English, a language still evolving, and considered unsuitable for serious discourse; the second, that the Charterhouse had notoriously poor internet access. The strength of the wireless signal would vary wildly throughout the day, for no reason on earth that Hume could divine. As a result, he had to keep a close eye on the signal strength bars at the top of his menu bar, and jump at any opportunity to consult Google, or Wikipedia, or Pliny's Naturalis Historiae Liber XXVII—XXXII.

Proceeding therefore in fits and starts, what should have been a two or three hour task (the essay is really quite short) took Captain Hume the better part of a day, so that by the time he shut the lid on his MacBook Pro with a weary sigh, the sun had long set, and a rumbling in his gut reminded him that he had neglected to eat anything since breakfast. He began to get out of his chair and head down to the Slug and Lettuce, when suddenly he was struck with a panicky feeling, the like he had rarely experienced since facing a line of Polish cannon. Had he remembered to save the document before putting the computer to sleep? He opened the laptop. Woke it from sleep. The document was there. It was safe. He had saved it.

Yes, he had saved it. (Would that Aeschylus or Sophocles had been so prescient!) And because he saved it, dear reader, Hume's essay can now be presented to you, in whole, unedited by any but its original author's hand:

On Exhaustion

One can without fear of argument posit, that there exist severall forms of exhaustion: these being spiritual, moral, physical, intellectual, and fake. Of the first two little mention need be made, as anyone who has experienced either will immediately recognize *"conditio, votum, cognatio, cultus disparitas...si sis affinis..."* about which the less said, the better. In my own particular *jardin des supplices* (*pace* M. Mirbeau!) there doth growe one or two daemonic subcultures, the which, if given proper physick, may some day flower in that YELLOW so feared by the writer of *La Fanfarlo*, and throughout historie has ever been given o'er to signify wickedness, in the works of Galen, Avicenna, Paracelsus, Laurentius, and Christopherus à Vega (*lib. 2, cap.* I), among others. (I leave out the copious references in the *Corpus Hermeticum* because, well, if you haven't so much glanced at the work of Trismegistus belike you shall disagree with my conclusions out of sheer casuistrical irony.)

Haply the reader has chanced to experience first-hand the next two — and by far the most common — forms of exhaustion: that is, the physical and the intellectual. The physical may have, as Sir Thomas Browne wrote (himself an excellent physician, as some under the thrall of his *Urn Buriall* are wont to forget), two causes: excess exertion, or excess of humour in the blood. Either should be treated with leeches, as soon as possible, the better for the purged system to reanimate itself. The work of Drs. Watson & Crick has proved, as timeless works have a strange habit of doing, that this practice is not only sound but based at the same time in the most ancient and modern realms of science, the which to say the science of IMAGINATION, where precision rules and fancy bends herself to her master's tasks, will-ye nill-ye. One need only look in Matthiolus's' fifth book of Medicinal Epistles, not to mention Antonius Musa, that wonderful doctor to Caesar Augustus, in his book which he writ of the virtues of betony, for confirmation of the principle of scrupulous adherence to *qui semel id patera mistum* and all that implies.

Of intellectual exhaustion, both the causes and cures are much in doubt, and yet it is with that particular malady I myself am most concerned, because it is that from which I now suffer, without the least clue as to why or how it was contracted, or how to rid myself of the thing. Hours upon end I have spent digging through my library, and yet nowhere in Jason Pratensis, Marsilius Ficinus, Melancthon, Silvaticus, (esp. his first *Controversy*), Hercules de Saxonia, Mercatus, Porta, Scaleger, Rhodiginus, Pentheus (*Bacchis Euripidis*), Vitellio, even good old Hippocrates, to mention but a few, could I find the answers I sought. I had hoped that completing the first thousand page draft of A *Secret Historie of the Voiage to Mickle-bury Land*, and then immediately undertaking my own "secret voiage" across the seas to the country of the Gauls, would prove a tonic for my depleted intellectual reserves. But none of that, marry come up! I am as empty as a rundlet of Barbados, and cannot fathom it. Haply I should have spent more than twenty hours every day for the past two months writing the *Secret Historie*; belike by drowsing the other four I so damped the fires of inspiration they have all gone to ash, and blown to the four corners. I am now consulting Burton's excellent *Anatomy of Melancholy* for some remedy, if not for my exhaustion, at least for the sadness it has provoked.

Of the fifth kind of exhaustion, which is to say, *fake*, one need only kick the scurfy impostor in some tender part, and hie him back to work.

The references to a thousand page draft of *A Secret Voiage to Mickle-bury Land* (likely Ireland) and a further voyage "across the seas to the country of the Gauls" (obviously France) are puzzling, because no evidence of either such a work or such a voyage exists. I think I would know if that evidence existed. I think, even if every trace of that evidence had met with History's eraser, I would still know. I would feel the existence of these things deep in the stitching of my self, somewhere.

Because we are the same person, Tobias Hume and me. There is no difference. I can look out my window at the Samuel Somers magnolia, or the towering white fir at the far margin of the hedgerow, and know the same things Captain Hume knew in his stone-walled room at the Charterhouse:

That I have broken every rule that was ever made, by Nature or Man. I have. The small hairs on the back of a fly I have plucked and used for toothpicks. I have driven through the sun without singeing my flesh; I have dive-bombed volcanoes with my fists. I don't pray, I beg. I don't stand, I sit. These are my two essential characteristics. If you know these two things, you know everything you need to know in order to classify me.

Winter's long embrace gives way to the cold fingers of spring. I am thorned, you know. Most of the time you only see my thorns, and these are enough to keep you away. Spring stretches everything, from length of day to spine of tree, we all grow taller and thicken slightly and in many cases froth into flower. Mine are amber-yellow, grown from Briar stock. I am hardy, but the soil around me must be kept well-forked. Do not so much as utter the name green-fly or caterpillar in my presence. These things are anathema.

Two children playing catch next door. A ball rolls in the road. The screech of tires. Mr. T. Geoffrey W. Henslow, M.A., F.R.H.S., cutting buds in his greenhouse, cocks his good ear, squinting, as if trying to see the sounds he thought he heard. He shakes his head to signify nothing, returns to his work.

The scent of blood reaches me at the gate of the white fence. From where I sit, laughing at fragile things, immersed in self-pity at my recklessness, my pride, the brevity of blooms, I see a piece of colored chalk that no one, now, will use.

O Tobias, how I miss you. Beneath the millipedes of thought, beneath the thundering elms, the trentaine of desperation... beneath all of this remains. The what remains. Sadness abides. So, too, does hope. Adieu.

Index:

intuitive, 104; and reason, xviii, 75, 79f, 113; and sensibility, 37ff, 52, 104, 113; with respect to the internet (not cited in text); pure concepts of, *see* User's Manual

The Hangover

SIDE ONE

1. Calling out in transit (4:05)

Sam Anonymous had a drinking problem.

*   *   *   *   *   *   *   *

Brown vinyl of the sofa peeled with sticking sound from humid flesh of back and legs as he sat up. Pattern of raised swirls on the vinyl were reproduced on skin: corresponding incarnadine impressions.

2. Your hate: clipped and distant (4:30)

Low whistle of kettle rose in pitch and volume to climax in piercing shriek that unmoored the murmur of Sam's thoughts. From tin of instant coffee he spooned quantity of dark powder. Hands shook slightly as he struggled to fill the cup with sour-smelling coffee. Scratched idly at the corner of one sleep-swollen eye: steadied himself against the counter. A ribbon of water lined the front edge of sink where he had sloppily rinsed the mug. When he pressed against the counter water seeped into the waistband of his boxers.

3. Martyred: misconstrued (3:58)

Her name was Violet McKnight. Five foot two in bare feet. Short hair dyed unnatural red swept back from lunar face: cranberry strands fell in her eyes when she made an emphatic gesture. Nose small, well-formed, eyes the color of root beer, narrowed to skeptical slits when challenged.

*   *   *   *   *   *   *   *

Spitting toothpaste into sink Sam noticed with equanimity that the spent paste was streaked with blood from his gums.

4. Not everyone can carry the weight of the world (3:24)

He was twenty-nine years old. In February he would be thirty.

5. Inside the moral kiosk (3:32)

A wave of nausea broke and receded. Sam hunched forward on the couch. Palpating his cheeks: annoyed by growth of stubble. Counting backwards could only manage four days before the fog of elapsed time refused to lift.

6. Shoulders high in the room (3:30)

Weaving unsteadily down the street, he saw her outlined against the black glass of her bedroom window, body limned by a nimbus of yellow streetlight.

SIDE TWO

1. Did we miss anything? (3:55)

Sam yawned, stretched his arms, stood and heavily walked across the room to turn over record. Returning to couch: revisited by a coil of his earlier nausea unwinding in his gut and feathering upwards through his chest. Unsnapped the cap from a plastic bottle on the table next to alarm clock, shook two aspirin into his hand, placed them with thumb and forefinger carefully in back of mouth, and swallowed with effortful gulp.

*   *   *   *   *   *   *   *

What use is experience without memory?

2. We could gather: throw a fit (3:18)

One thing at a time: watching Violet bend towards him by light of a guttering candle.

3. All nine yards (3:05)

Scratched his hair in imitation of thought. Hoisted himself off the couch and began sorting through pile of clothes on ugly square of brown-and-white carpet.

Love is a crazy and unkempt thing that grows like a wild weed in the heart. It will suffer the cruelest attempts at eradication with quiet strength, and will take root and prosper in even the stoniest soil. True love, like true art, admits no moral influence. Had he read that or was it original?

4. Shaking through: opportune (4:30)

In frustration he ripped the front buttons and stripped off the shirt: left hand got tangled in the cuff: which he had abstractly buttoned moments earlier: and pull as he would: flap as he might: the shirt refused to let go. Sat down on the couch: head in hands, the tattered shirt trailing to the floor like captured flag of some defeated army.

5. Up the stairs to the landing (3:01)

World adheres to stringent rules of form and content: these rules, Sam knew from prolonged contact with books, were not frangible. Just as a story must have beginning, middle, end, so a soul must have one body to inhabit. Proliferation of the soul's forms would mean rewriting rules of human contact.

6. Long gone (3:17)

The wind picked up and there was a smell of rain. Sam buttoned his overcoat with reddened fingers. The tips of a succession of telephone poles flecked the sky on the far side of the broad avenue: up one of these scrambled two squirrels.

Dark tracery of oak limbs: russet and orange and mustardy leaves: cold rain-scented air: combined to form an impression of remote beauty that reinforced and focused his sense of longing.

Continued past a brick house, windows ardent with citrine light. Fragrant gray smoke curled from its chimney: leaves of a silver poplar fluttered in the wind, undersides flashing white like a flock of luminous moths: from thick tangle of azalea bushes came sounds of a small animal scrabbling for food or shelter.

Fine rain needled his face but he did not mind the wet because in his heart he carried a word —finally! — that was the word he needed. He held the word before him like a lighted candle to ward off the rain, and the cold, and the black despair of night as he walked towards Violet's house.

CLEAN

— *Medium High*

In Bloom

Under An Azure Sky<<not crazy about the title, a little pedestrian for the piece? How about Under A Coincidentally Yellow Sky? Joking, of course, but what about that title? Agree. GOOD TITLE TK

Even impatient people won't get bored watching the Damask rose; and sick people will find its blossoms cheering. The location of the flower depends on where you are, physically, and the politics of self-destruction.<<what about getting rid of the comma after *are?* OKAY When Routledge Ruut stood, alone and smoking in the middle of the desolate battlefield, he could not see the parts of bodies or writhing and groaning formerly//recently? YES. BETTER. human* forms, he could not see or hear anything in fact, blind from the blood caked over his eyes and deaf from the cannon's shout, but he could see in his mind the *Rosa damascena* he had grown in a small clay pot on his windowsill earlier that year.

Who was Routledge Ruut kidding? That rose was long bloomed, and the clay pot shattered or consumed by fire when the <<delete AGREE enemy troops ravaged the town near six months ago. And yet. If a thing can be held in the mind and regarded with precision, passionately held by force of will as if the eye were present, he had been taught, then no separate reality existed which could overthrow the one so constructed.

What you wouldn't do to get there. The carnage before you: a drop of elderberry jam on a snowy mountaintop. Routledge Ruut, you are a killer. Probably** makes you feel better to say warrior, soldier, but that's a sham, sham, sham. <<for some reason the three shams feel less impactful to me than just one. AGREE The roses you seek: nothing will stand in your way. No one can or will. You start wars, and you end them, all for the sake of a rose. More precisely: for the attar that can be obtained by steam distillation in copper tubs of crushed petals and sepals, the olive-green, malodorous oil, from roses harvested before dawn and distilled the same day.

After which, what happens? More roses grow. You can't stop them from growing. When they grow, you go after them and slaughter anyone who stands in your way.

Everybody wants my blood. The helicopters shooting diamonds above the low hills at night, the Russian nurses, the white-coats, the sloppy sailors with buckets of fish guts, preening*** on the wharf. Or perhaps I should say: there's no one who does not want my blood. Not the inmates downtown in their leather cell, sitting side by side by side by side, not the loser seagulls, not the seeing-eye toadies who peer through slats at time of day.<<only instance of slightly rote imagery SEE YOUR POINT. MAYBE CUT THIS PART AND FOLLOWING SENTENCE, GO DIRECT TO "THAT IS WHY…"?Not one of these does not want my blood. That is why I am covered in bruises, from needles, from constant poking with needles. That is why I am so bloody anemic.

Routledge Ruut has pig snot for brains. What runs through his arteries I wouldn't even guess, but nothing good. Nothing pure. Once I saw him pricked with a small sword and something olive-green spurted from the wound. I will admit that I wounded him. For what reason he does the ravaging and so forth. For what reason at all. The countryside is stupid, infested with stupidities, plied every day with more stupidities, through various means, some popular**** and open and free. Routledge Ruut knows all that, but he doesn't care a damn except for the wellbeing of his roses. In the meantime I am running short on blood, and there are only so many stupidities I can reasonably stand.

I need to stop Routledge Ruut. Well, not stop him but instead turn his attention[a] to the stupidities. From the roses to the stupidities, which are like roses in that there is no end to their blooming. But someone like Routledge Ruut, not some one like him but him and him only, because there's no one like Routledge Ruut, should his warlike spirit be properly directed, or better put focused, could stop the stupidities. Could attack them with his curved sword — there's an exact word for the type of sword Routledge Ruut uses, perhaps the word is scimitar, perhaps not — and decollate the stupidities, blood spurting in rufous fountains over land and sea and high into the oxygenated sky, past gravity's pull, through the atmosphere and gathered in ruby globules by the flexibly inflexible rules of physics, floating forever in vast: space.

But a man who bends his mind to roses is not easily swayed. Il n'y'existe pas un homme qui can resist the lure of botany — the sweetest science, super-succulent and dangerous to the sanity. Jag alskar dig, spoke Karl The Father. Contrary to expectations, he lived a mostly placid and self-satisfied life, crowned with crowns, and in addition had interests outside botany extending even to anthropology — the science of cartoons. One does not contradict§ the other: existence and non-existence. These are complementary ideas, even necessary ideas, albeit frivolous and entirely beside the point of what Routledge Ruut would call "bleeding." Everything about Ruut was a hybrid. The man himself — his ridiculous name — blends seeds of meaning and matter into new, unimproved forms, because he can't leave well enough alone. And yet he searches restlessly for a perfection in nature that he cannot find in his artifice; will kill anything that tries to block the pursuit of his silly blooms.

In this way death came to our town.

*Theory of constraints and all her applications. Tic-toc. Toe. Toe explains all in a pretty little bundle of joie. Wagon-lits. Carte paths. For all thy protestations to the contrary, sir, 'tis enow that we twain d'accord the propre ceremoney o'er the matter, and out on't, fogh! Cat's paw and cat skills and cat o' nine lives growling like weed in the hothouse of terra cognita. 'Sblood and 'Sbody and 'Shair and 'Sface and 'Sveins: we shall one and every follicle belike transvoorted to the Viking press of the moon, hear me, hear ye. Crag-faced in the rocks owing to excess of rundlets, owing to stony silence, owing to the sea-craters I haply misericord to bottom.

**Fear not the wroth of vermiform signs or songs, my dear kunsthalle; ohrwurm; baublehaus. Underscan my stayings, and prithee forgimme. I have been the blackell of apathy, friends, it is a place none should after see. A dark ocean on a dark night, fingers of sea-foam ringing my neck while I bipedal nautically to fins of strings. Look up at pinholed, pinwheeler sky! It is no blanket but a rush of invisible gas to the end of ends. No monsters lurk, and none underfoot, howsomany fathoms ever you durst. No monsters anywhere but dear. Monsters are not cheap. Immensities of mind. Pilules for compelling rod-on. Two or three choses that je sais about Hell. A season deferred. In Hell. From Hell. To Hell. Every demon you have ever seen dwells inside you; you worship him as you worship yourself. Hell itself is no dwelling-place, but a location nonetheless: a very rental in the soul. The Virgin Spring. An urgent urge, demi in the dusk, from minuit to minute, or smaller still, and quite quiet. Ouphe in the forêt, train-sported with circles of merveilleuse ochre and rose, rising, with slow care, towards Bedlam.

***Northing. Naxalite violence. Any port or prince in a storm. I have made pacts with an adze that will shake the plates and rain devilish on the flimsy city. Horrors will multiply like human cells; divide and resupply. You have not seen death like I have seen death because you look with sightless eyes at sightless eyes. The stench of decay starts in living bones, spreads by lies and betrayal to the dead. I will tell you what is truth: truth. I will tell you what is beauty: beauty. I will tell you what is death: death. Power corrupts; absolute power corrupts, absolutely, but also murders without second thoughts. Without remorse. Any vengenace-minded God is riddled with remorse, but not these.<<agreement? Meant to refer to "second thoughts." I'm flexible on this.I am the I am.<<cut? Stronger to end with the vengeance-minded god? parody of a Biblical reference. Me likey.

****Darkness inside the muted light of sunset: when you stand in front of the window and stare at the far hills. These are the bad angels, gathering in gloomy bunches like poisonous grapes, parmite with blood. The leafless trees scratch with upstretched arms at scudding clouds, and in the growing mist barn owls perch on lower branches, scanning the radio air for the slow heartbeat of approaching doom. The bad angels grasp in their grasping claws the agenda of nightmares, larded with entrails of dead shrubs and bits of styrofoam and brick. You roll the heavy door across its track and fasten tight the locks. You know that nothing made of something can stop the angels, who are nothing. You've looked them in the eye and seen the end of time, and the end of time was a mirror. And still you roll the door, and still you light the fat candle, and the wax drips forest green on polished marble floor: you turn and find yourself inside a tomb, which is where you keep the rain, for safety.

But you are not safe. The rain cannot keep you bright for long, and your tears will only fall, unseen. There are corridors in this place that lead to holy places, but all the holy places have been destroyed, out of love, out of a desire to love that burns without burning — a plague of love, a cholera of kindness. Dig a ditch and wait for pistol shot in back of neck. Or is that too romantic? Would you prefer a meaner death? Shriveling for years in the data basement, in an old hard drive, dispersing bit by bit on the ocean floor of knowledge, frozen, unexplored, blind, pressed flat by calamitous gravity.<<beautiful section

ªThe Periplus and Rhapta. Arab and Indian traders looking for gold in the first of twenty long centuries. Is this what you mean by Africa? The devil is no fool. Why fear the means of grace, expel yourself from your own garden? Difficult to till, ravaged by bad angels, daily exposed to the secrets of flight. You think because everything has roots that nothing can fly? The last thing out of the chest, children, was a very fragile creature, its tiny hairs still slick with afterbirth. You must do your best to keep it alive.

§ thursdygurl44 (*3 hours and 2 minutes ago*) Im sick an tired of the ignorant morans commenting here who don't HAVE THE FACTS!!!!!!

Fables of the Deconstruction

Rufous Knicks, rampant in blue serge suit and hairs-cut, stepped down the wobbly back shell of Forever Corner like a king descending to court. That or another like sentence would mark well to begin this history in old days whereof I have understood some, having lived for petty times in that epoch. I do not possess any old days books, but have had opportunity to peruse precisely two at cabinet of Mme. Pi and on one occasion had extinct pleasure to listen Super My Love read the first chapter of a leafy tome encased in papery sleeving, color pale green, entitled *Lol*. In which I comprehend was a lacrosstick of some nature in which I cannot decipher. A lacrosstick occurs when letters stand around for longer words in which the writer does not wish to unveil for private reasons.

The reading of the old days book *Lol* was a magic. It is different to hear words in the head of you than bespoke by another. O man I have found. I retain no or less memories in which I was young, in which without doubt my mother or some person would have read at high voice from old days books, once I have been told in which were plenty abundant.

I return to Rufous Knicks putting the feet forward and again forward in back of Forever Corner until he had reached the door to the fence at the limit of the garden. I find tiresome to describe every action of Rufous Knicks when I already know where he is going and when and many details concerning his destination. Nor would it be just as interesting to arrive properly without malingering on the travel? Then. I will omit from here to there.

Rufous Knicks entered the building through blown-apart front. Had arrived by straightforward route. Rufous was not the kind to take laborious mappy when the straight line could be put in place end over end in which you can finish by arrival. Inside the building birds bunched on attic rubble at the far end waiting for something. These birds did have bad blood in them, or appeared. But Rufous unslung his rifle and made as if to shoot at them, but the birds did not wow or flutter, but continued to wait only for the something. Black eyes followed Rufous as he forwarded through the main hall and up the stony staircase, mightily damaged but not fallen, into the upstairs room where Madame Salamander Pi held her cabinet on most mornings and some of the afternoons.

Madame Salamander Pi was a gross person. In this way she demonstrated her superior skill-set in the department of living, and was awed by others who had no comparables towards acquiring sustenance and in which consequence were meager in size. Certain, Rufous was twangy in which comparison to Mme. Pi. But he had a compensating vigor but an excellent aim with respect to his rifling but a speed and range of motion but was difficult to tackle. Had he the knowledge of keeping things for long times no one doubts whereby he would on the other hand challenge Mme. Pi for the charge in which she held.

He had no complaint or intent to challenge in mind today's morning, but Madame Salamander Pi could never know this advanced of the moment, and so her aides dispatched themselves to greet Rufous Knicks before he could attain the threshold of her cabinet. These were two name of Sham and Polish but, in no which gross, still you could say largely in frames.

"What is your business with Madame Salamander Pi?" asked Sham.

"I wish to ask her advice on a project of mutual beneficence," said Rufous Knicks.

He struggled in the grasp of meaty claws but not too much.

"I do not understand these words," said Polish, or Sham.

"I have a desire to confer with Mme. Pi. It is a matter she will understand but I do not think that you will, judging from the lack in which you have lately demonstrated ensuing from my prior words."

"We will have to ask Mme. Pi, or the patron, as we call her, if she wants to conference with you," said Sham, or Polish.

Rufous Knicks indicated that he understood this act as a necessary, and would wait in the grip of only Sham or Polish while Polish or Sham performed a liaison with Mme. Pi.

While Polish or Sham was gone Sham or Polish said to Rufous "I hope you do not understand our actions to be a counter-temps. It is a duty that we must convey as part of our boss."

"I confess a petty perturbation, in which is not your fault, and do not blame you," said Rufous. "My argument is with the order of things. As much with the crows and this exploded wreck as with any person."

"What you say to me is not meant for me, in which it is okay for me to hear, but your talk is one-sided and does not require a response," said Polish. Or Sham. "Here is Sham or Polish, come from Mme. Pi, the patron,
with informations."

Sham or Polish rejoined his colleague and said to Rufous Knicks, "Mme. Pi has interest in listening to you, Rufous Knicks, if it is not a trouble to come with us to her cabinet."

"It is not a trouble," said Rufous Knicks. "Let's go."

I need not add that I have only imaginaried the talk between Rufous, Sham, and Polish, as I was not present and did not have afterwards a chance in which to unpack the exact wording of the exchange from Rufous, as he lay dying.

I will now indicate the camber of time by use of an eclipse.
….

Rufous though mortal of wounds made strong effort to retrieve his corpse to backyard of Forever Corner, at which one saw each other as I marched my circle of deliverance the daily pain. I found him slouched against the wall at step bottom.

"What has passed?" I asked Rufous, who though smeary with blood and shallow respired, had no look of great trouble on his visage.

"Your head," joked Rufous.

"I mean in really," I said.

"There was disaccord between me and Salamander Pi," he said after a while and with some difficulty.

"Of what nature?"

"Of a nature in which she had a mistake of my intent, in which I finished on the wrong side."

"Well obvious," I said.

"I have a secret I would like to tell you, now that I am dying," said Rufous Knicks.

"Tell me your secret, Rufous," I said.

He made a clan of eye and motioned by which I should come closer.

"A knowing hole of great significance has been opened. I think that Salamander Pi has recognition of this hole, and will take steps to control the results. You must fill your lack, in which you have no fault, to the best delay. Salamander Pi cannot take consequence of the fruits of the secret."

"I wonder myself that I have in no sense understood your import," I said.

"I will ask a small favor of you."

"It does not matter what."

Rufous Knicks smiled in which his teeth were not seen. He spit on the ground and there followed either a laugh or a cough or a laugh in which became a cough.

"You have ever been a good friend," he said. "Truth, I crawled back here and waited in hope of your arrival. I had a luck."

It was a trouble to put my attention in the direction of Rufous Knicks' purpose, because I was rapt by the seeing of cracked skin around his sharp knuckles. The skin itself looked a separate organ to the underlying bone and filament, undulant independent of hand movement, as if possessed of intelligence its own.

Having essayed some further paroles, Rufous Knicks ceased to inspire. In agreement with his ask, I did not attend to dispose of his corpse but passed to the voluntary in which he had given to me instructions very specific.

I will now indicate the camber of time by use of an eclipse.

Second-Hand Blue

I'm going to meet my death on the Rue du Nil, in Paris, in exactly one hundred days. The Rue du Nil is more an alley than a street, and dead-ends at a brick wall. There are no windows or doors at street level anywhere near the wall. It's the perfect place to trap someone. To trap myself. To die.

You might reasonably ask, "Why such measures? Yes, you drugged and raped a thirteen-year-old girl decades ago, but those were crazy days, there were mitigating factors, and in the years before and since, your contributions to world culture have been of such magnitude that they overwhelm that grievous lapse. Do you really feel so guilty, even now, that you want to die?"

I don't want to die; and I don't feel guilty. Not for that incident, anyway. As for the arguments regarding extenuating circumstances and the value of my work, these are things lawyers and critics, or to be more and less precise, judges, must consider, but not me. I am going to die because I have to die, and I will die in the Rue de Nil because that is where my destiny waits, impatiently, and one cannot outwit destiny.

My biography is incredible, even to me. The things I saw as a child, the things I did as an adult: horrible, wonderful, horrible, but useless. Perhaps inevitable, perhaps even necessary, but useless, all the same. Because in the end I am going to die, in a cobblestoned alley in Paris, in the small hours of the morning, at the hands of an imaginary mob. Should they carry torches? I haven't decided. Torches might be a bit much, but the lighting would produce a nice effect. Shadows on the wall, marching inexorably closer. Shot correctly, edited properly, the scene could be marvelously suspenseful.

But then it would not be true, and death must always be true. Quick, merciless, and banal. I will crouch in fetal position, bunching my tiny frame in what will look like infantile terror, wearing borrowed jeans and a sea-blue windbreaker with a broken zipper, and pray for a painless demise. I don't believe in God, but I predict that I will pray, nonetheless.

I'm not telling you my fate to elicit pity, nor do I want anyone to try to talk me out of going to the Rue du Nil on the appointed day. I'd be especially miffed if someone were to try to intervene and prevent my death. *Inutile*, anyway, because you don't know when I'm writing this, so you can't know when my hundred days are up. Could be tomorrow. Could be a hundred days from now. Or any day in between. Could, quite obviously, have already happened. My advice: leave me and my death alone. It's a personal matter. It doesn't concern anyone else.

I will share with you a story that will help you understand. It's a story no less for being true, and it's true no less for being set far in the future. The closer I get to death, the clearer the future becomes. I've always had a knack for seeing ahead, as well as for seeing behind. But I've never before seen ahead with such clarity, whereas my view of the past has become distorted by the stained glass of memory. Have you noticed that if you stare at anything long enough it loses its apparent quiddity, and transforms into a mirror?

*

There are one hundred varieties of love, and five hundred varieties of hate. These are exact numbers. I've spent my life calculating and tabulating these varieties, so you can be assured of the accuracy of my headcount. Do you know the song "Thin Line Between Love and Hate"? Beautiful song, except: wrong. There's no line between love and hate. It's like crossing the border from France into Switzerland by train. No one checks your passport, there are no customs officials to search your luggage, but you are in fact changing countries. Whole sets of laws and regulations and cultural mores and even languages alter invisibly, and if you put one foot wrong you end up in jail, or in a spacious and comfortably-appointed chalet.

It's the same with love and hate. You cross the border from one to another unaware that anything's happened, and nothing, really, *has* happened, except that everything you say and do is now governed by a completely different set of rules, and enforced by a different authority. This can be bewildering, and just as with my entirely fictitious France/Switzerland example, you can end up in a kind of jail for no sensible offense.

Ignorance of the law is no excuse! How many times has this bromide been repeated by a sententious robed figure sitting on a high bench above a cowering culprit whose so-called crime was having once, years ago, picked a small flower with delicate blue petals that grew in abundance in his own country but which was, all unknown to him, a rare and protected species in this foreign place. No matter that he picked the flower out of love, and gave it as a gesture of love to a dear friend. The friend had been mortified, had blown the whistle (in this country everyone carries whistles), and he had been forced to run from an angry mob bearing pitchforks (it was daylight, so torches would be absurd).

Because there are five times as many varieties of hate as there are of love, it would seem to follow that it is easier to go astray in that vasty dark country than in the relatively small, sun-dappled land of love. However: no. Hate, a product of misapplied reason, is a lawless and anarchic state, whereas love, ruled by rigorous passion, has had to develop a complex and even contradictory set of regulations, and its borders are not clearly marked. And because it's a much envied and sought after destination, it is strictly policed. Let me illustrate.

*

1. The Country of Love, Part One

As Anna drew close to the earthberg certain features became clear. Giant scars along its face, vertical rakes as if by talons of an impossible bird. Evidence of great impact along the shore. This was no easy landing, thought Anna. We felt the shudder in the village. The Elders knew what the shudder meant, though to most they did not explain, or gave some other explanation. There was a secret vote. I was elected. The election was presented as a choice, but I had no choice. Not inside me, where the choice had been made long before I was elected. I had a sense of: finally. She may count herself lucky who just once has contracted the purposefulness that makes life and death worth bearing.

Nearer the earthberg Anna lost perspective and could not gauge its mass, though more details emerged. Trailing ropes. Ladders hammered into jutting rock. A horizontal maple. Here and there, the glow of some kind of light from within some kind of cave. Wondrous beyond imagining. A hive thrumming with unseen activity.

Anna approached a semi-circle of poles on which had been hung lanterns, signaling the end of a long, similarly-lit boardwalk that led to a small entrance at the foot of the earthberg. Three men stood in the pool of lantern-light, their shadows long and inconstant.

"I'm Anna," she said, upon reaching them. The men had unreadable expressions, neither hostile nor friendly nor exactly neutral.

"Most likely," replied the largest of the three, in a thick accent Anna had never heard.

"I've come from the village through the woods," she said.

"Does the village have a name?" asked the large one. "We were just discussing, Pyotr and Nikolai and me, what part of the world we might have stumbled upon."

"We've always just called it the village. But I have heard some of the Elders use the word Norfolk for the larger area."

The large one snorted. "Norfolk. That's of no use. There's a thousand Norfolks, and most of them aren't even in the north. Not anymore, at least."

"Please, sir, might I ask, how many are in your company?"

"You speak a kind of Anglo," the large one mused. "Which means, as I was telling Pyotr, we might be anywhere."

"Sure enough we're somewhere," interposed the one who must be Pyotr.

"I am called John," said the large one. "We travel with one hundred souls, though we started with five hundred. Many of us are sick, and we are in sore need of fresh supplies."

"Might I come on board your ship?"

The three men began to laugh.

"Ship!"

Anna smiled, perplexed.

"This hunk of rock's no ship, kid, we cannot steer nor guide her. We call her *Quoi qu'il en soit*."

"Then you are Franks."

"No, we are *Rus*. *Quoi qu'il en soit* is Frankish, yes. Its name in our native language... I don't even remember. Anyway."

"Is there water here, and food?" asked the one who must be Nikolai.

Anna did not answer. Instead, she turned to look at the boardwalk. "Might I come on board?" she repeated.

"Where are my manners?" said the one called John. "We may

be scavengers, but we're still men. Follow the lights to old Tom. He'll take you topside."

A mountain is most impressive from its base, thought Anna. At its height you lose the majesty. And the threat, however ridiculous, of being crushed.

At the end of the boardwalk was a metal door with a small window, lighted from the inside. A man's face appeared in the lighted window, startling Anna. The door slid open, heavily, and she found herself staring at a small, thin man with a heavily creased forehead. He wore jeans and a faded blue windbreaker with a broken zipper, and was covered in dust from the crown of his dusty curls to the scuffed leather of his dusty workboots. When he smiled his skin cracked, and in the cracks was more dust, and dust between the gaps in his brown teeth.

"Going up?" he asked.

"I think so," said Anna.

"There is only up." He stepped back from the door and motioned Anna inside. "My name is Tom."

Anna walked through the doorway, into a very small, dimly-lit metal room. "I'm Anna," she said.

"Anna," repeated Tom. "Hello, Anna." He pushed a button on a panel near the entrance and the heavy door slid closed with a satisfying clunk.

"Hold on," said Tom, pressing another button on the panel. There was a loud creaking noise, and the whirring of gyros, and the room lurched upwards at a frightening speed. Anna cried out and ducked to the pimpled metal floor, clutching a handrail. She pulled the hood of her blue cloak, borrowed from her sister, over her head.

2. The Country of Hate, Part One

A clot of darkness inside muted light of sunset, just above the far hills. These are the bad angels, gathering in gloomy bunches like poisonous grapes, purple with blood. Leafless trees scratch with upstretched arms at scudding clouds, and in the growing mist barn owls perch on lower branches, scanning the radio air for the slow heartbeat of approaching doom. The bad angels grasp in their grasping claws the agenda of nightmares, larded with entrails of dead shrubs and bits of styrofoam and brick. You roll the heavy door across its track and fasten tight the locks. You know that nothing made of something can stop the angels, who are nothing. You've looked them in the eye and seen the end of time. And still you roll the door, and still you light the fat candle, and the wax drips green on polished marble floor: you turn and find yourself inside a tomb, which is where you keep the rain, for safety.

But you are not safe. The rain cannot keep you bright for long, and your tears will only fall, unseen. There are hallways here that lead to holy places, but all the holy places have been destroyed, out of love, out of a desire to love that burns without burning — a plague of love, a cholera of kindness. Dig a ditch and wait for pistol shot in back of neck. Or is that too romantic? Would you prefer a meaner death? Shriveling for years in the data basement, in an old hard drive, dispersing bit by bit on the ocean floor of knowledge, frozen, unexplored, blind, pressed flat by calamitous gravity.

The Periplus and Rhapta. Arab and Indian traders looking for gold in the first of thirty long centuries. Why fear the means of grace, expel yourself from your own garden? Difficult to till, ravaged by bad angels, daily exposed to the secrets of flight. The last thing out of the chest, children, was a very fragile creature, its tiny hairs still slick with afterbirth. You must do your best to keep it alive.

3. The Country of Love, Part Two

The elevator shuddered to a halt, and the heavy door slid open. Tom gestured for her to exit, and Anna stepped onto a flat, barren surface, mostly red dirt, cratered in places, sparsely grassed, with a few sickly ash trees. Under one of these, a hundred paces away, gathered twenty or thirty men, women, and children, listening to an Elder with a scarred and wrinkled face, long white hair, and a scraggly, untamed beard. She went closer, in order to hear.

"In with the good, out with the bad," the Elder was saying. "But it's not air of which the teacher speaks. Something more valuable. Essence. Out with ignorance, in with wisdom. Knowledge of the self means knowledge of things hidden in plain sight. When you can see what's in front of you, these hidden things will be revealed. When you let out what is in you, that is creative. Held inside, these uncreated forms living in darkness will consume you like the fires of hell.

"The aspirant must work in solitude, because only then comes the ability to know yourself. Without distraction. Without guidance, except that which answers the bell of the mind. The two words which interest us most are therefore *gnosis* and *logos*. *Gnosis* translated as insight or vision, and *logos*, as proclaimed by the teacher, who reserves the term for himself, represents the highest form of being: truth.

"Did we create the sun or did the sun create us? Or did something else create both, or have we always existed, but in different, possibly less cumbrous, form and content? Or — do we exist in different form even now but lack the means to see? If you do not know the manner of your coming you cannot know how to go."

The Elder caught sight of Anna lurking on the fringe, and stopped talking. Everyone turned to look at her. A murmur of curiosity spread through the crowd.

The Elder held up one hand for silence.

"A guest! Welcome! By what name are you called?"

Anna was disconcerted to be addressed directly, but stepped forward.

"My name is Anna. But I'm afraid you're mistaken. I'm not a guest."

"What, then?"

Anna opened her borrowed cloak to reveal a heavy vest of some explosive, wired together and attached to a detonator, which she now held in her right hand.

"I was elected by the Elders of my village."

No one moved, or seemed particularly alarmed. The Elder sighed.

"I see. May I ask why?"

"We have a book," replied Anna. "It contains our laws, and prescribes certain actions that we must take to preserve ourselves."

The Elder nodded thoughtfully. "We, too, have a book, which foretold your coming. It's called The Book of Life. Does your book have a name?"

"Usually we just call it the Book. But I've also heard it called the Book of Love."

She shut her eyes and pressed the detonator.

4. The Country of Hate, Part Two

Everybody wants my blood. The helicopters shooting diamonds into the bluffs at night, the Russian nurses, the white-coats, the sloppy sailors with buckets of fish guts, preening on the wharf. Or perhaps I should say: there's no one who does not want my blood. Not the inmates downtown in their leather cell, sitting side by side by side by side, not the loser seagulls, not the seeing-eye toadies who peer through slats at time of day. Not one of these does not want my blood. That is why I'm covered in bruises, from constant poking with needles. That's why I am so anemic.

Thomas Quin has pig snot for brains. What runs through his arteries I wouldn't want to guess, but nothing good. Once I saw him pricked with a dagger and something green spurted from the wound. (I will admit that I pricked him.)

To what purpose he does the ravaging and so forth? To what purpose at all? The countryside is stupid, infested with stupidities, plied every day with more stupidities, by various means, some popular and open and free. Thomas Quin knows all that, but he doesn't care a damn except for the well-being of his flowers. In the meantime I am running short on blood, and there are only so many stupidities I can reasonably stand.

I need to stop Thomas Quin. Well, not stop him but instead turn his attention to the stupidities. From the flowers to the stupidities, which are like flowers in that there is no end to their blooming. Thomas Quin, his warlike spirit properly directed, could stop the stupidities. Could attack them with his curved sword — there's an exact word for the type of sword Thomas Quin uses, perhaps the word is scimitar, perhaps not — and decollate the stupidities, blood spurting in rufous fountains over land and sea and high into the oxygenated sky, past gravity's pull, through the atmosphere and gathered in ruby globules by the flexibly inflexible rules of physics, floating forever in vast: space.

But a man who bends his mind to flowers is not easily swayed. *Il n'existe pas un homme qui* can resist the lure of botany — the sweetest science, super-succulent and dangerous to the sanity. *Jag älskar dig*, spoke Karl The Father. Who, contrary to expectations, lived a mostly placid and self-satisfied life, crowned with crowns, and in addition had interests outside botany extending even to anthropology — the science of cartoons.

The one does not contradict the other: existence and non-existence. These are complementary ideas, albeit frivolous and entirely beside the point of what Thomas Quin would call "bleeding." Everything about Quin is a hybrid. The man himself — his ridiculous name — blends seeds of meaning and matter into new, unimproved forms, because he can't leave well enough alone. And yet he searches restlessly for a perfection in nature that he cannot find in his artifice; will kill anything that tries to block the pursuit of his silly blooms.

In this way death came to our town.

*

I hope that my brief sketch of your future — which could just as easily be your past, I'm no longer convinced there's a useful distinction — shows you why I have to go to the Rue du Nil in one hundred days and meet my destiny. Everyone deserves to die, and everyone will die. It's a question of when, that's all. I've lost track of how many of the one hundred varieties of love and five hundred varieties of hate I have tasted, and in tasting violated; but what's the difference? It only takes one.

The Ordinary Rendition of Caeli Fax

Thomas Early's window faced east, so when he was working at his desk in early morning he had to draw shut the gray linen drapes. There were nonetheless gaps where the fabric billowed or buckled. He bent his head forward to avoid the probing shafts of sun that threatened his concentration. He wrote quickly but with great care. Because he was left-handed, he had through long habit developed a method of chirography that neither smeared nor slanted.

The sooner he finished, the sooner he could leave. Not just the sour milk apartment, but the city itself. Its bleached buildings: tallow-faced ossuaries of history. He would escape, hurtling down the highway toward the stone house like a satellite across the starry cope. Exiting, he would navigate quickly the back roads near Commentry and Reblog and Twithe, because he knew every curl and coil, and which were likely to be corked with slow tractors hauling bales, and which were likely sheets of verglas. His late model Utero possessed startling efficiencies of fuel, without—without!—sacrificing speed nor power. Under two man-made hours he would be there. The gravel driveway blanketed by rufe and citron leaves. The wet crunch of rubber on pebble as he braked to a stop.

"Trotting on to net a porter right now," thought Thomas, though he had no idea what the words meant. Was this a message from Caeli? Or a stray transmission from the radio air?

He was unsure what to do for a moment, and for a moment his pen stopped moving. He straightened in his chair. Looked over at the clock on the wall, sighed. Bent forward and started writing again.

In a faraway woods, nestled in a feathery white fir, Caeli Fax awoke, suddenly aware of a cone pressing into the small of her back. She fluttered to the forest floor, brown needles matting the loamy earth, through which nonetheless poked hundreds of green ferns. Her workboots made no noise on the bruised needles or broken twigs in the undergrowth as she walked. Her dress snagged on a holly bush, but she continued, and the bush relented without complaint. Nor was any harm registered by the strange fabric of the dress.

Past the mossy ruin of the old watermill, evidence of human resistance, evidence of futility, of abandonment. The river changed course over not much time. Remained only a shallow stream several meters away, near-buried in upgrowth of bunchberry and wood-sorrel. You can hear more than see it, though there were gaps that glinted darkly in the early light. Hints of water, really. Astuces. What you do with these your own business.

She hoped that Thomas would remember everything she told him. He had a very good memory, but still. At the end of the day, or the beginning of a new one, everything written is a kind of translation. Even with your own hand: translation. And most of the time that's okay, you live with that. But these last words were vital, fidelity paramount. Did she trust Thomas? As much as she trusted anyone, which is to say: no. The world of men had not given her much reason to trust. Even before World Fever, when people were generally less panicked (though still panicked) and selfish (though still selfish), she had been betrayed more than
many times.

Perhaps it has to do with my insubstantiality, thought Caeli, walking towards the ecotone. A few cattle with tan hides and occasional dirty white blotches nosed through the clover and tall grass in the pasture. The edge of the sky, fulgid with rising sun, was streaked rose and tangerine behind wisps of cloud. Mist pooled around the grazing cows. Their pale ruets *making music*, as Fiat used to say. Unself-consciously, sloppily, the gentled fruit of millennia of interference.

I look at the natural world and I can't see the natural world, she thought.

I will go to the old stone house and wait. [*Ðæt mon agefe ðæt lond inn higum to heora beode him to brucanne on ece ærfe*]. Phrases in old languages come without bidding into my head, because I have lived too long. Thomas talks about the radio air, but I've been hearing voices long before that invention. Before any invention. Or discovery, as most things are more properly called.

It's odd, thought Caeli Fax, that at this time and in this place "hearing voices" should be a sign of mental illness. Most of history would have made of you a prophet or a poet. Most of history would have genuflected before you. Which, frankly, can become tiresome. The life of an oracle is not for me. You can't go anywhere. You have no privacy. Everyone is always asking questions. The wrong questions, or worse, questions without an answer, or with so many answers you have to just pick one at random.

No one asks anyone questions anymore. Instead they ask everyone. They consult the crowdsource for information and auguries. The questions never change, nor the answers. But the entitlement, see, now that's new. The self-satisfaction. The pride. Well, why not? You'll be dead enough soon enough.

She had reached the loose wire fence at the end of the meadow. The fence was supposed to be electrified, as a warning to the cattle not to stray, but none of the fences were electrified anymore. She climbed over and then through the drainage ditch and onto the smooth red dirt alongside the road.

An old man in an Alpine hunting cap walked along the road with his retriever. The dog heeled sharply as the man in the cap tugged its leash. Wait for me to pass like I'm a danger, a careening car, the (shapely) figure of death.

"Hello," said Caeli Fax to the man in the cap.

The man in the cap nodded curtly but said nothing in reply. Caeli looked the dog in the eye and smiled. Her teeth were small and perfectly formed, stained yellow from tobacco. The dog stared big-eyed and panting at Caeli, straining slightly at the black leather leash attached to his collar. The dog wanted to go closer, but the man in the cap would not let him. The dog wanted to inhale more deeply the wood-scent, the odor of centuries. But the man in the cap wouldn't let him.

He never had before. Last chance, thought Caeli, as she continued down the road towards the old stone house.

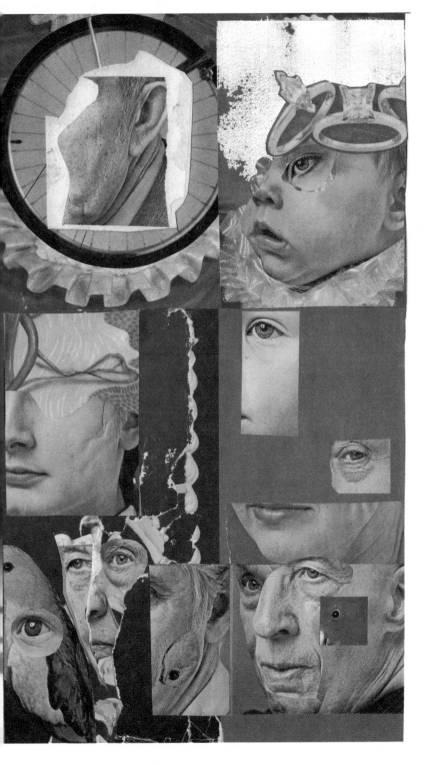

Chapman's Green Hairstreak

Even the sun runs late in Paris. In the pre-bloom dark, from an unshuttered window five stories above the street, Thomas Early could hear the Turks on the sidewalk arguing about attar of Damask rose. In Turkey the production of attar is strictly regulated by a state-run collective, but these guys were rogue producers, distilling in moist cellars the fragrant oil that had, in the past, both started wars and ended them.

But now the world was coming to a natural conclusion, so the arguments that drifted on currents of metropolitan air to Thomas Early's ears were not merely pointless (they had always been pointless) but distracting. He had work to do. He had to finish his manuscript. The subject of his manuscript was "The hardened sap, or gum resin, excreted from the wounds of the American Sweetgum," but the important part, the part that had to be finished before the moon's day dropped, was a record of the last words spoken by Caeli Fax before she zipped back to the sky.

Thomas turned away from the window and moved towards his desk, which was really a table, made of black alder (*Alnus glutinosa*) taken from the pilings of the now-collapsed Rialto in Venice and varnished dark brown. Before serving the Rialto the wood had been chopped from a copse in Clapham Commons and taken from there to Brighthelmston for use on its famous pier. But the pier, in fact a disappointed bridge, was already finished, so the wood was shipped to Italy. How it came to the atelier of Jakob Friedlander, *ébéniste*, in the 4eme arrondissement in Paris is a mystery, and possibly a scandal.

The table was piled with books and a confusion of manuscript pages, all covered in Thomas Early's tidy handwriting in black ink. He was wearing a dark blue polo shirt, short-sleeved, and black tennis shorts. His hair, cropped closely and without care, was dirty blonde. He was tall, 188 centimeters in his bare feet, and he was barefoot. His curiously ovoid face was covered in a week's worth of stubble, flecked with gray, and his small watery blue eyes were set back in their orbits, so that it was difficult to detect movement of corneas. His eyes had an acuity of 50 cycles per degree, which gave Thomas an extraordinary ability to distinguish fine detail from long range.

The room was small, approximately five meters square; and on the floor lay a faded 17th century Persian rug of excellent design. The light from the table lamp spilled over into a silvery semicircle on the rug, revealing an intricate rosette pattern that, although Thomas did not know this, predicted with uncanny accuracy not just his future but all of his futures. The tightly-woven wool fibers of the carpet comforted his feet the way a sweet caress will stop a lover's tears, in Norse mythology (see: *Helmskringla*).

We had always had hopes for Thomas Early. We had thought he'd be the one to stop the spread of World Fever, to find a cure, to save us. If anyone could, it would be him. We had not considered that, having found the cure, he would refuse to use it. That he would refuse to save us. Out of love. Out of the kind of over-whelming love that offers insight, that understands: the cure is not a cure.

The intervention of Caeli Fax proved crucial in this respect. She explained to Thomas Early the disastrous effects a plague of love would have on the human race; that far from mitigating World Fever it would in fact drastically increase the speed of its spread. Thomas was not easily persuaded, but because his mother had known Caeli's aunt in their shared hometown — Dayton, Ohio — he at first granted her his attention and after some time his trust. She brought him books: Burton's *Anatomy of Melancholy; Blanchot's L'arrêt de mort*; a biography of Salamander Pi. These were useful in his work, and too expensive for him to buy. She would arrive after midnight, and Thomas would light two fat candles (a gift from the Ecuadorean writer Charles Panic) that were now little more than hard pools of wax with furled edges impaled on the rusted wrought iron candle-stand (a gift from Oscar Delacroix). Thomas and Caeli often talked until dawn, or until Thomas fell asleep, at which time Caeli would slip out the window while Thomas drowsed, slumped in his leather club chair.

Caeli was slim, with delicate features, and graceful hands that she rarely used to emphasize a point. She would lay her left hand on Thomas' table, lightly drumming, and occasionally wave a lazy finger through the nearest candle's flame. Her right hand rested on her knee. Her large, long-lashed eyes, caramel brown with flecks of green, seemed black by candlelight, and sparkled when she talked, and sparkled more when she listened to Thomas talk. Most often she wore a tan trench coat over a blue cotton belted V-neck dress, and heavy leather boots with laces, though she would sometimes show up in old jeans with a white blouse, untucked. Thomas thought her very glamorous, precisely because she lacked any pretense to glamor. That she was not human only added to this perception. Her black hair was cut boyishly short, and she smiled often, which softened the angles of her pale face.

Her voice was light, especially in contrast to Thomas' rheumatic rasp, which for some reason had only deepened and thickened when he quit smoking, two years earlier. His septum had cracked in a snowball fight when he was eight years old, and never healed properly; as a result his nose was visibly crooked, and he had chronic rhinitis which, compounded by an allergy to dust mites, had eliminated seventy percent of his sense of smell.

If only one of those compacted globes of winter had not made contact with my face, at such a time, in such a way. Maybe now, all these years later, I would be able to breathe.

If you could build a time machine, by which I mean another time machine, obviously, would you go back and dodge that calamitous ball?

Most of the conversation between Thomas and Caeli was conducted in French, because they both felt more comfortable, or more at home, at least, in that language, though it was not their native tongue. "We are both exiles," Thomas had remarked, early on. "Everyone is an exile," said Caeli.

We had first begun to notice World Fever at the end of the last century, though at first we misunderstood both the symptoms and their underlying cause. When, a few years later, *Under An Azure Sky* (Expanded Edition with Notes) by Eddie Incognito was published, it was widely ignored. Thomas had been staying near Nice back then, looking for the poet Gardner Stout, who was rumored to be living in an old farmhouse in a small hamlet somewhere in the neighboring countryside. He read Under *An Azure Sky* in one go sitting under the glossy leaves of a strawberry tree on the edge of a meadow and immediately recognized its importance. Within a decade, everything Incognito outlined in his book would come true. Within fifteen years, we would all be infected. World Fever is that powerful, that attractive; no one stood a chance. No on except Thomas Early. That, at least, was the hope.

Having finished the book, he put it aside and lay down in the shade of the small tree. He noticed a butterfly fluttering around the tree's hermaphrodite, bell-shaped white flowers, and recognized it as a Chapman's Green Hairstreak. Watching the little green imago, he realized that Gardner Stout must be very close. But he no longer cared.

That was probably a mistake, Thomas considered, sitting down at his table and shuffling some papers, looking for the heavily marked-up Wikipedia printout about the Rose of Castille. Gardner Stout had many bad qualities, but he would have recognized the importance of *Under An Azure Sky*. And unlike me, he would have done something about it.

As No One Lay Trying to Die

Or help us knowing ouch has dropped a stone upon
our headlines. Or scare me up inside, the backend of
troubles unimpressed.

***

These will prep the churchy masses and the desperate tryst. I
sold the rest stop and I told the best stop and I stop and stop. These
our American rhythms. These our God bless you platitudes and God
bless you. Please.

Sonorous tones. Sonorous tones. Sonorous tones. Said the bell
to the town. Send your meat to my seating plan. Uncannery rows
of raw chair in canteen disciples. That is more than. Sky goes up to
other sky and looks in his sky and sky says blue.

Spell it out, watery Gravesend. Say we lay him under, say the
infallible foe curtails his trip. Throw the most. The most just. By
half, in half. By this rod or that rood. This main thing. This willing
feature. Excerpted file. Slingland. Chalk-lined and visible along
the pitch of channels one two three and even four. A dish nosed
south on a clear sky. The winds: sirocco, marin, leveche, xaloc,
tramontane, mistral. All corridors lead to katabasis, from Alpine
droits to Massif slips. Down, downy, soft into underworld. We
used the Socratic method on a couple of local wines, and brake
bread and blood of Christ was everywhere. Pooling in the dirt and
possibly this dirt was the same dirt. Wash the red from the tide, no
reward ever warrants the present.

***

Then when time stutters, muttering obscurantist, and you've
chaussed and rumbled hoofing it big time into ass-bag of a rue
aboard your moto and howsoever on account wherefore of quantity
of lyeserge sloughing down the straw veins in your stuffed suit
and—the helmet, you forgot, you always forget—so that encounter
(inevitable, ineluctable, unelectable) of flesh-meets-brick Hello!
Hallo! Helloo! Showy slo-mo smacking, deliquescent bone through
the frayed pull: I Am Flying impossible I Am Flying untrue I Am.
That I Am.

Strange does not begin to descry. Vetting will commence in tea
minus milk, sugar, spoon. A nursery of stares in the vault of Helen
shows, per aspirin, a bastard tune. Light from headspace, fluting a
dead hurt, on the run from run off. Spare me, beggar. That wood.
Bee. Absence of nonsense from common sense. Lightful. Set of sun

from lavender wist to blood orange and rose, heaving, from twilit death to moony height. Abandon all soap. Scrub pine and never, never. Beak in, beak out, beak on or haply dose. Her thymes are not yet loam, nor lonely roan. Cancreous encrease by bushel or farthel, we all say the same but we all hear the hippy parse. Lou! Stay. From purse into lapping dog, huge among us will be willing. Yew? Ash? My crew is askance.

***

The only useful thing that anyone can do, put together two or three strings and call them Paragraph: but that which has been driven LEEWARDS by the windows of MEANING will have forever inked upon his brain the last rights of man! But bottles and bottles are courage for the children of victory. It wears on its shoes its badge of things that were. Who wouldn't age rapidly in however much an atmosphere? Trouble trunks, that. Places we've been. If these crossroads were splayed like Jesus. The machine makes them, you know, but not any more. Whole town's gone to seed. Have you any tea, dear? Have you a plea bargain at the flea market? My favorite is a kind of leaf that has to be plucked in the feather of its youth. Punched in the face like a bowl full of dreadful. Has to go where has to be. Are there any questions?

There can be no more questions. A drink for all sins. That one cost a bad penny but the true cost of any string cannot be measured by the toes nor hung from missiles; nor used like these cardigan buttons (from the front) nor stacked like firewood (on the porch).

***

Damn the hell out of any wight says contra, he can't know the extent of the problem. Bunches of liars growing like water-weeds on the actual planimitrie. Rufous, wide, and sky. Three colors of the body, when he lies there and lies. No one ever wants to leave, just like no leaf ever wants to turn, and none of the people or trees are fond of falling, adamsend or evening twain, crossed in the hairs of a simpler gun. All avenues embrouch now on the single road to night. Twixt here and there's a slippery pope benedicting the masses, and the chorus, and the versus. A modicum of modesty, if it please you, sir. 'Sblood! 'Sblood everywhere! The sayers of a thing must needs be brief. Luther's inkwell shrives all sins but leaves a blushy stain upon the red right hand of the object of his wroth. That's the question troubles me. That's the question. Not existential disparity, nor bipolar theorem, nor the set of ones. Nor zero. Nor the arrow.

A passing cloud obscures the source. Still there, obnubilate. Which is not to deny individual consciousness—merely to suggest that a single ego does not and cannot exist without the sum of all individual egos, and that from an infinite perspective, that individual ego is weightless and insubstantial—a tuft of feathers floating in the celestial ether.

Throw away the clocks. Flatten the keys. Hey, mom, don't feel too bad. Tonight before crispness —throne fires, pinecones wilding down the firecat lanes like average birds—I saw the word.

And the word was made flesh.

Invisible Ink

The settled fields no longer give. Black as monks' cowls the poppies yield, and blacker still the vegetable debris pecked by iron birds from under the vast heap of sunlit dust. Black clouds obscure the skies. *Whatsoever thy hand findeth to do, do it with thy might.* Who musters the daily storm in the murdering arm of the law? In the tenements of Kiev exist grandmothers who have lost everything more than once. Their hands are black from hoarding coal.

Down from Kazakhstan, the straits of Bosporus provide the only route for Caspian tankers. Winding through Istanbul from the Black Sea to the brighter Mediterranean like the distance from dark to light in Rembrandt's oils. Dozens of ships are lost at the blind turning where the sinuous river narrows to seven hundred meters. Their cargo leaks by metric tons into the inky water. (A waiter in a coastal café dims the gaslight to enhance the mood.)

At the center of every conspiracy lies a breath of hope. From the Latin: To breathe together. (*Com + spirare*) Hope's always borne from darkness, reaching towards a light not yet created. The blunders of God's secretaries have been well documented: Northrop Frye, C.C., B.A., M.A., LL.D., D.D., D. Litt., D. de l'U, L.H.D., D.C.L., F.R.S.C., who looks, in a picture taken seven years before his death in 1991, like a man who has stared into the abyss and found nothing interesting staring back, spent a good portion of his scholarly energy mining the Bible. Among other felicities, he describes how a Latin pun in the Vulgate turned The Tree Of The Knowledge Of Good and Evil from (probable) fig to (impossible) apple. *Malus/malum* is the least of its problems, but Frye was no mere pedant. A disciple most explicitly of Blake, he finds revelation in Revelation. Human creativity has in it the quality of re-creation, says Northrop, of salvaging meaning from the alienation of nature. "I make all things new": 21:5. Revelation's the inner truth of what happens in every human soul, every day — or rather outside of every day, since real vision must dispense with time. *Man creates history as a screen to conceal the workings of apocalypse from himself. We have to fight our way out of history and not simply awaken from it.* Apocalypse — revelation — is the way the world looks after the ego has disappeared.

God is not a circle—because a circle replaces eternity with infinity, and God comprises both and neither. Let us now consider trees: Of apple, and fig, and weeping willow, whose bark provided aspirin to dull our earthly aches, of ash, of oak, of palm, of Joshua and Judas, of the *Magnolia grandiflora*, Samuel Sommer, developed as a hybrid by the Saratoga Horticultural Society of Saratoga, California, in 1961. Described as "sturdy, leaves large, very glossy and prominently veined above, rusty-brown hairy beneath; flowers to 14 in. across, tepals 12, in 3 tiers of 4." Note the transposition of letters in "petal," the date of birth, the temperature outside, the blades of grass that poke through dirt at its base.

On July 14, 1912, Herman Northrop Frye was born in Sherbrooke, Quebec. He lived through two World Wars, saw the ashes drift from Krematorium II in the suburbs of Oswiecim, the piles of rusty utensils which were all that was left of the essential belongings of Jews taken by the Germans upon arrival at the camp, sorted, and placed in large warehouses in a section of Birkenau nicknamed "Canada" because it was a place of abundance. Frye lived all his life in Canada. He was appointed a Companion of the Order of Canada in 1972, for his insightful commentaries on Canadian culture (*par ses analyses pénétrantes de la culture canadienne*). His bibliography was abundant: he wrote twenty-six books and edited fifteen, contributed essays and chapters to some sixty more, and wrote articles and reviews for scholarly quarterlies numbering in the hundreds. Nothing he did made any difference.

James Greer is the author of the novels *Artificial Light* (LHotB/Akashic 2006) and *The Failure* (Akashic 2010), and the nonfiction book *Guided By Voices: A Brief History* (Grove Press), a biography of a band for which he played bass guitar. He's written or co-written movies for Lindsay Lohan, Jackie Chan, and Steven Soderbergh, among others. He is a Contributing Editor for the *Los Angeles Review of Books*, and plays guitar and sings in a new band called Détective after the Godard film of that name.

ZERO FADE A novel by Chris L. Terry

"Kevin Phifer, 13, a black seventh-grader in 1990s Richmond, Va., and hero of this sparkling debut, belongs in the front ranks of fiction's hormone-addled, angst-ridden adolescents, from Holden Caulfield to the teenage Harry Potter." **—Kirkus Reviews** *(starred review)*

Thirteen-year-old Kevin Phifer has a lot to worry about. His father figure, Uncle Paul, is coming out as gay; he can't leave the house without Tyrell throwing a lit Black 'n' Mild at him; Demetric at school has the best last-year-fly-gear and the attention of orange-haired Aisha; his mother Sheila and his nerdy best friend David have both found romance; his big sister Laura won't talk to him now that she's in high school; and to top it off, he's grounded.

TOMORROWLAND Stories by Joseph Bates

"Tomorrowland is a revelation, combining slightly skewed or fantastic conceits, a darkly comic tone, and wonderfully nimble, funny prose, all in service of a surprisingly serious, touching vision. These inventive stories mark the debut of a major talent." **—Michael Griffith,** author of *Bibliophilia*

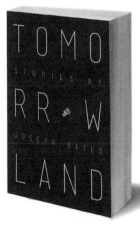

Joseph Bates's debut offers stories full of strange attractions and uncanny conceits, a world of freakish former child stars, abused Elvis impersonators, derelict roadside attractions, apocalyptic small towns, and parallel universes where you make out with your ex. At its core, the world of *Tomorrowland* is our own, though reflected off a funhouse mirror—revealing our hopes and deepest fears to comic, heartbreaking effect.

www.curbsidesplendor.com